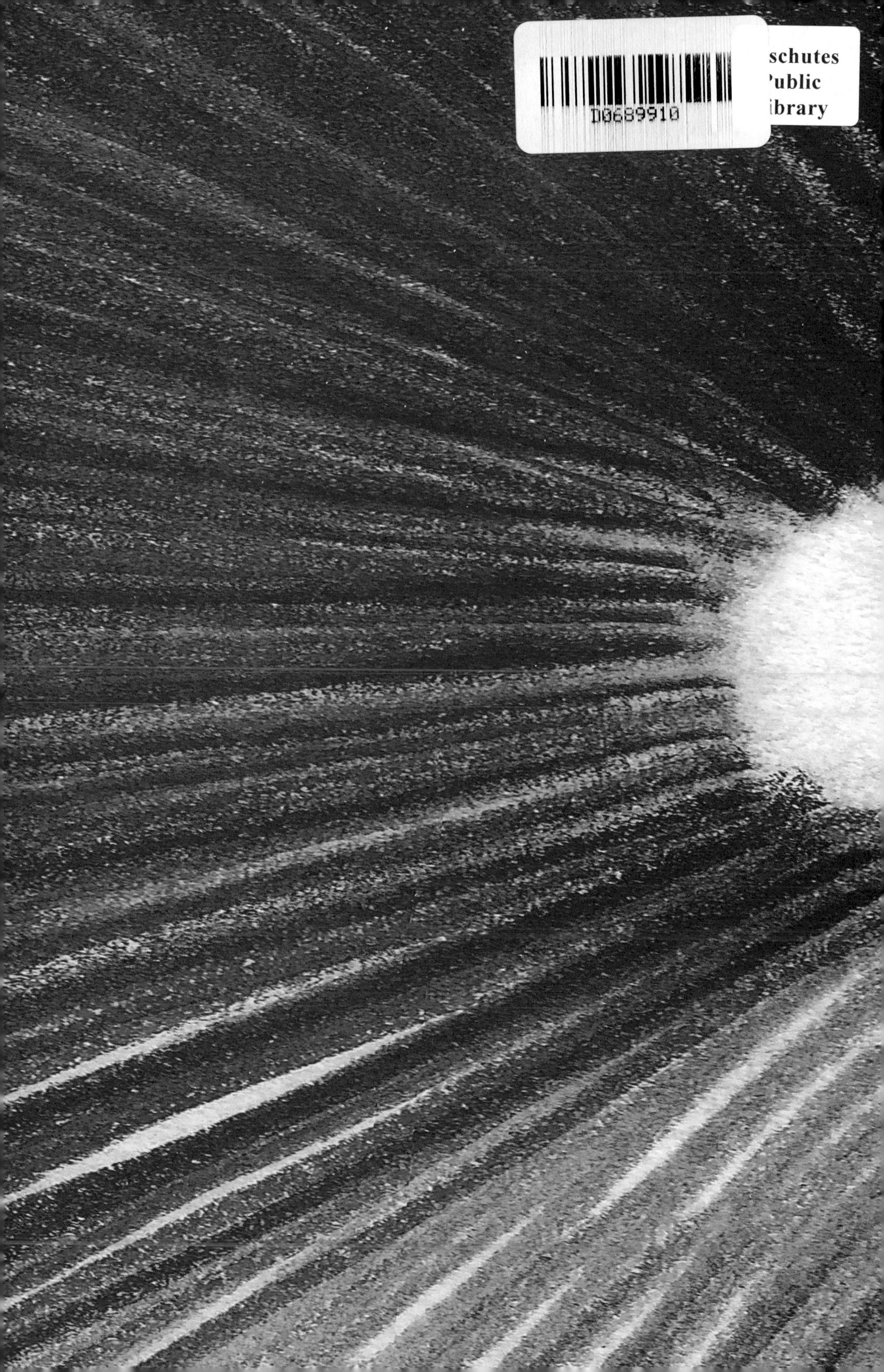

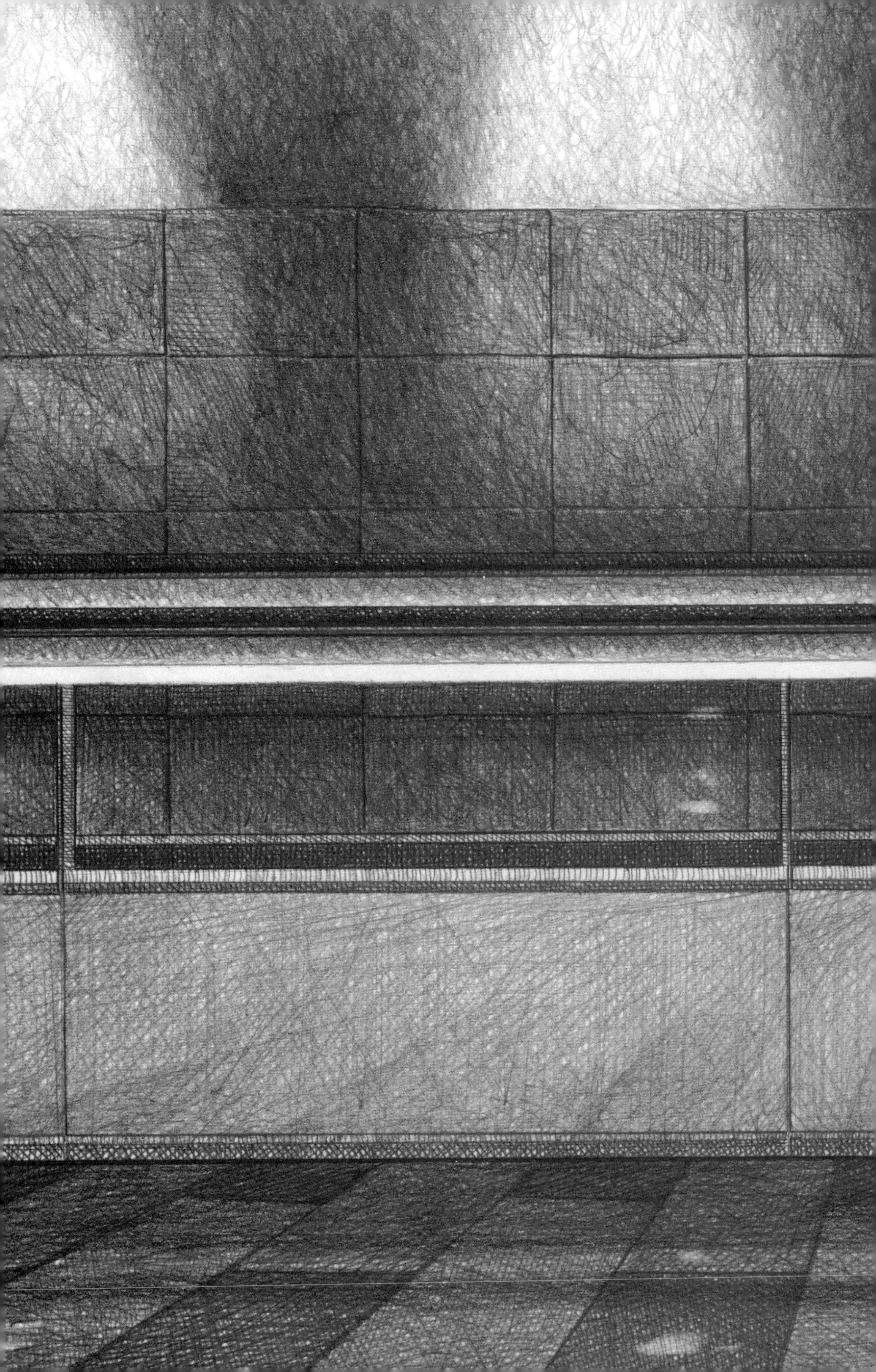

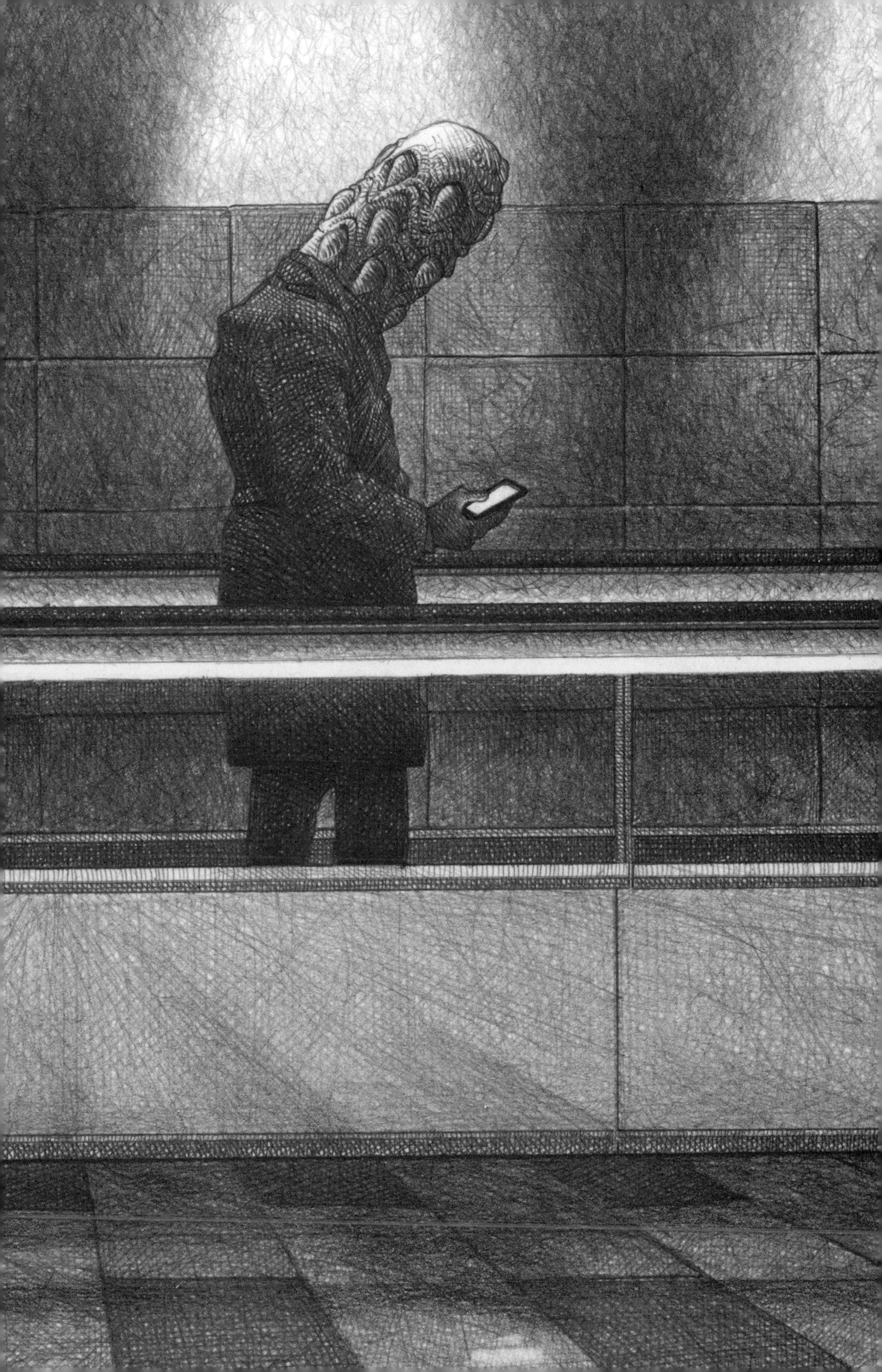

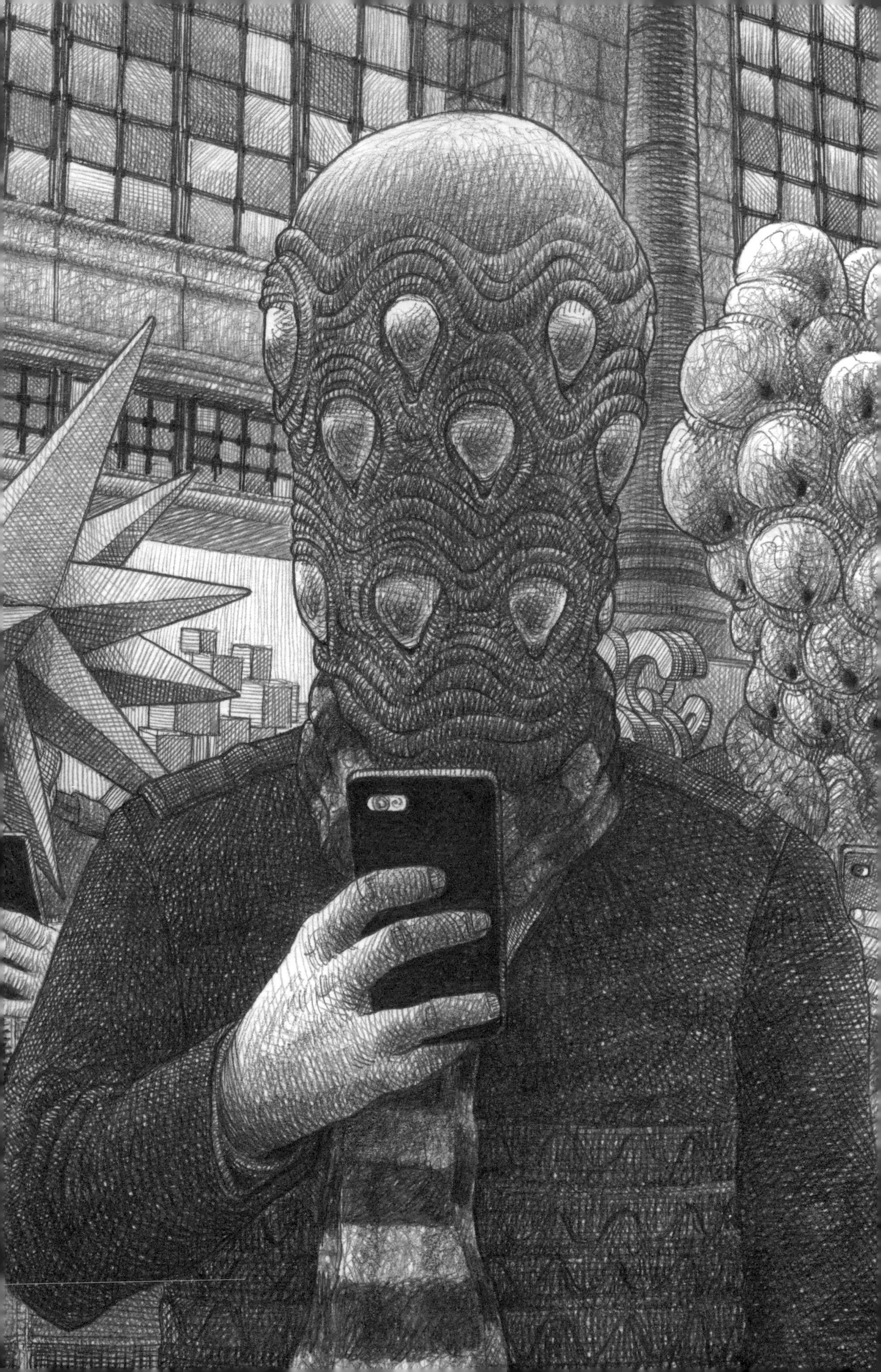

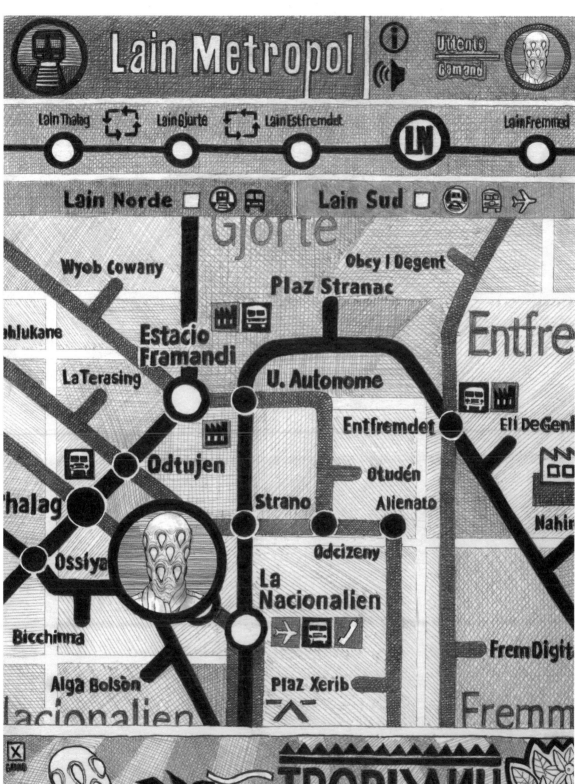

Lain Metropol

Uttente Gamand

Lain Thalag   Lain Gjorte   Lain Estfremdet   LN   Lain Fremmed

Lain Norde   Lain Sud

Gjorte

Wyob Cowany   Obcy I Degent

Plaz Stranac

ahlukane   Estacio Framandi   Entfre

La Terasing   U. Autonome

Entfremdet   Eli DeGent

Odtujen   Otudén

Thalag   Strano   Alienato   Nahir

Ossiya   Odcizeny

Bicchinna   La Nacionalien

FremDigit

Alga Bolsòn   Plaz Xerib

acionalien   Fremm

TROPI꞊ANU VA꞊AMSI

CLIKÉ

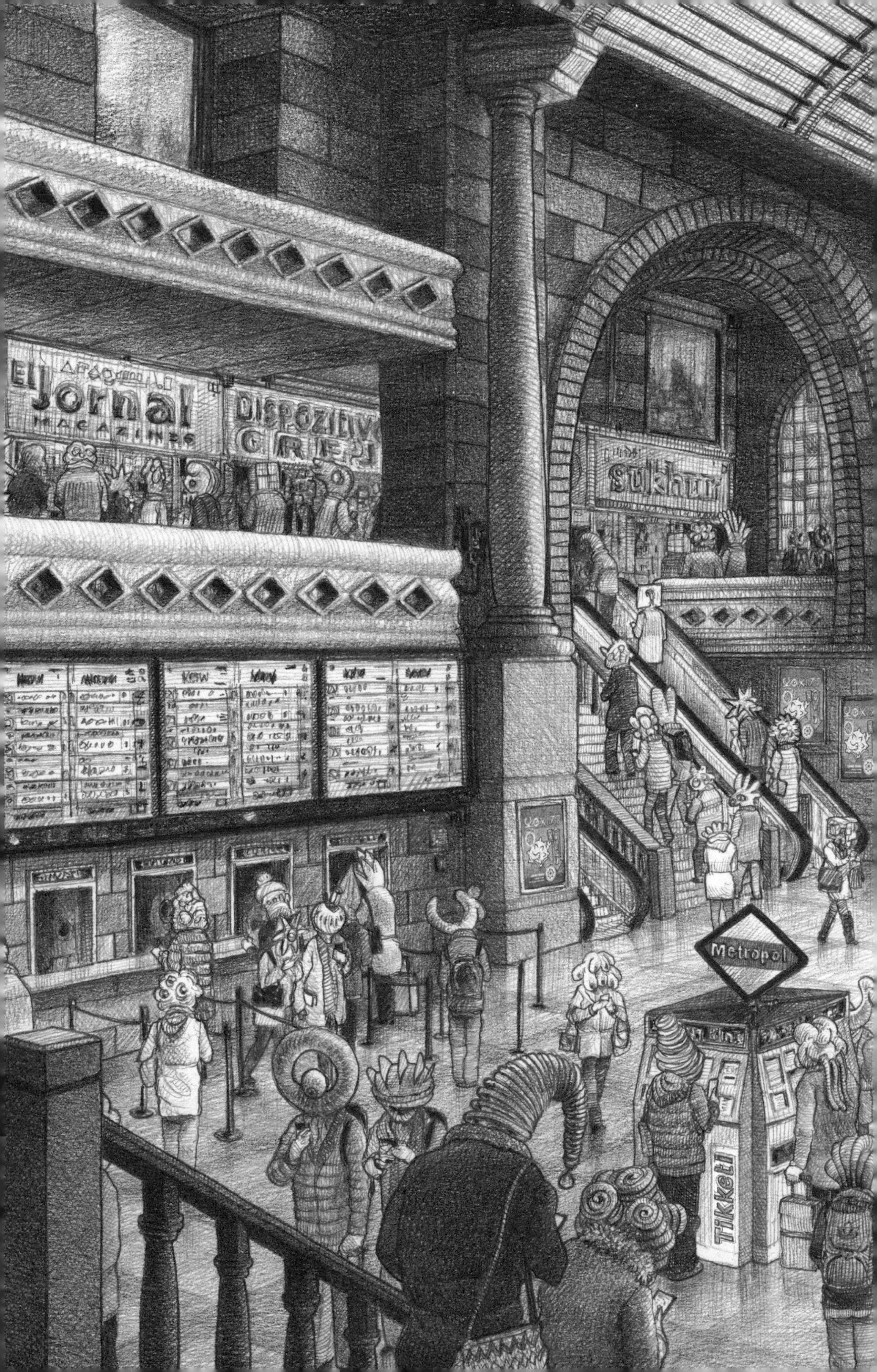

El Jornal
MAGAZINES
Metropol
Tikketi

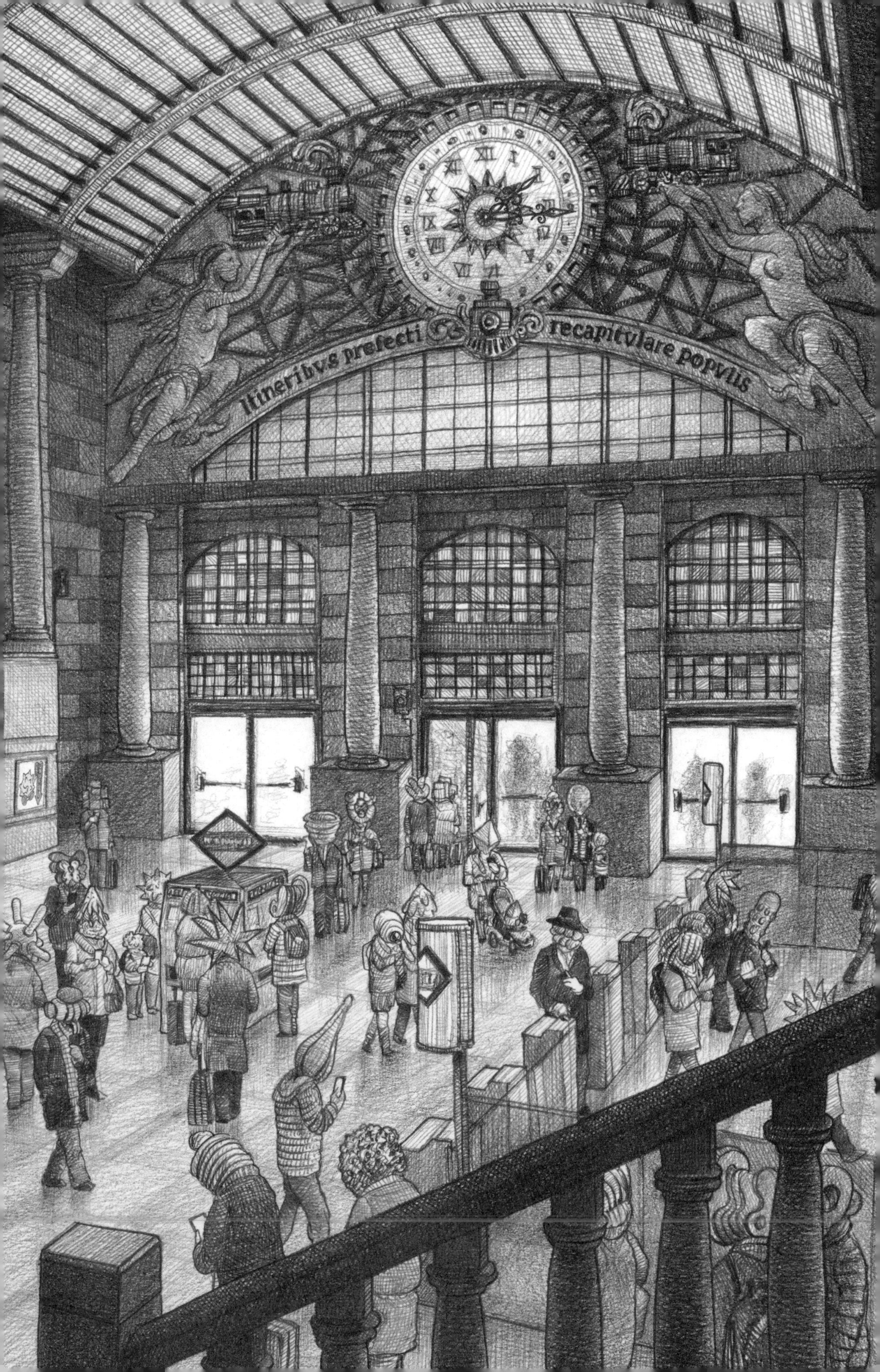
itineribvs prefecti
recapitvlare popvlis

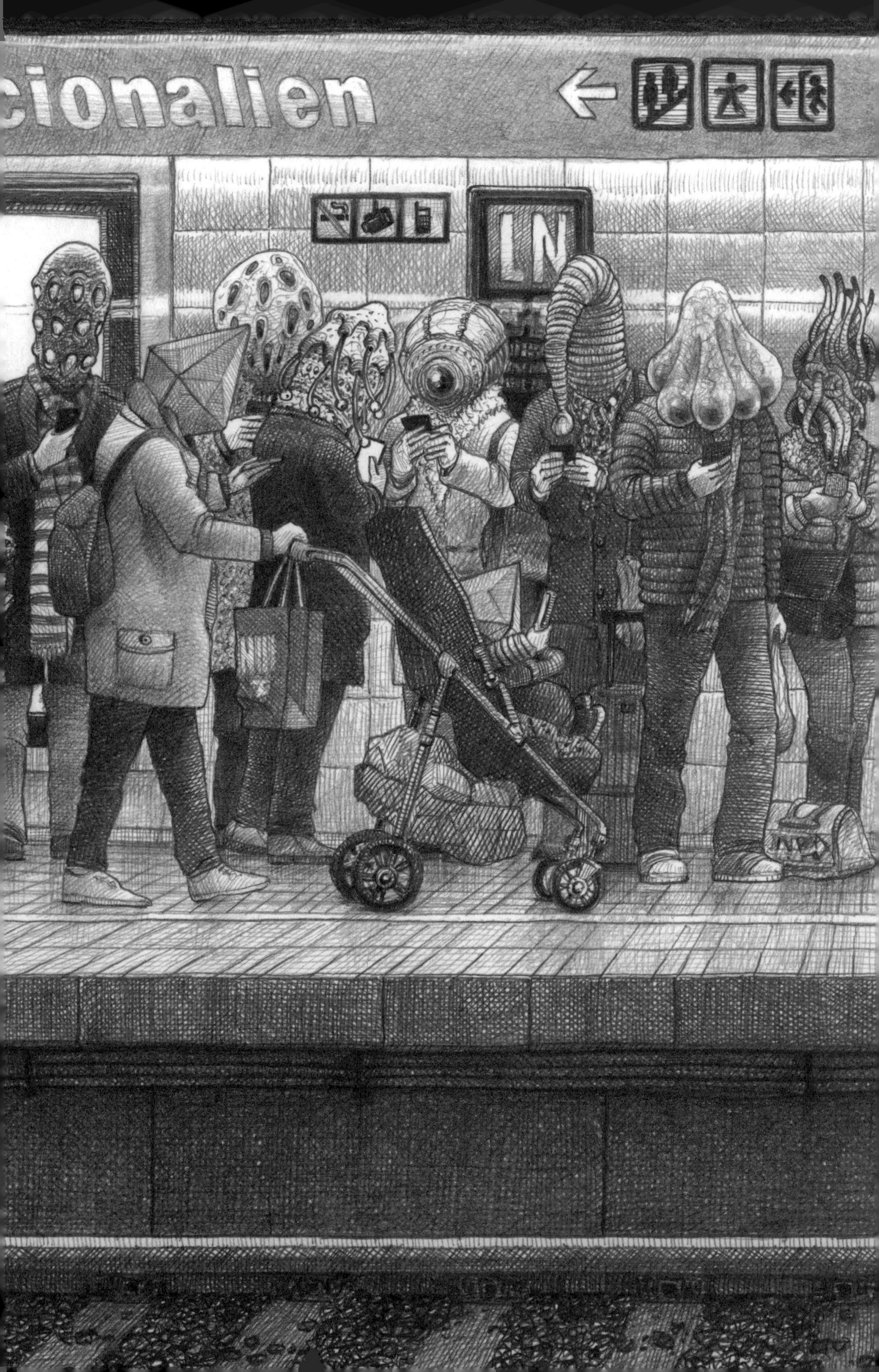
cionalien
IN

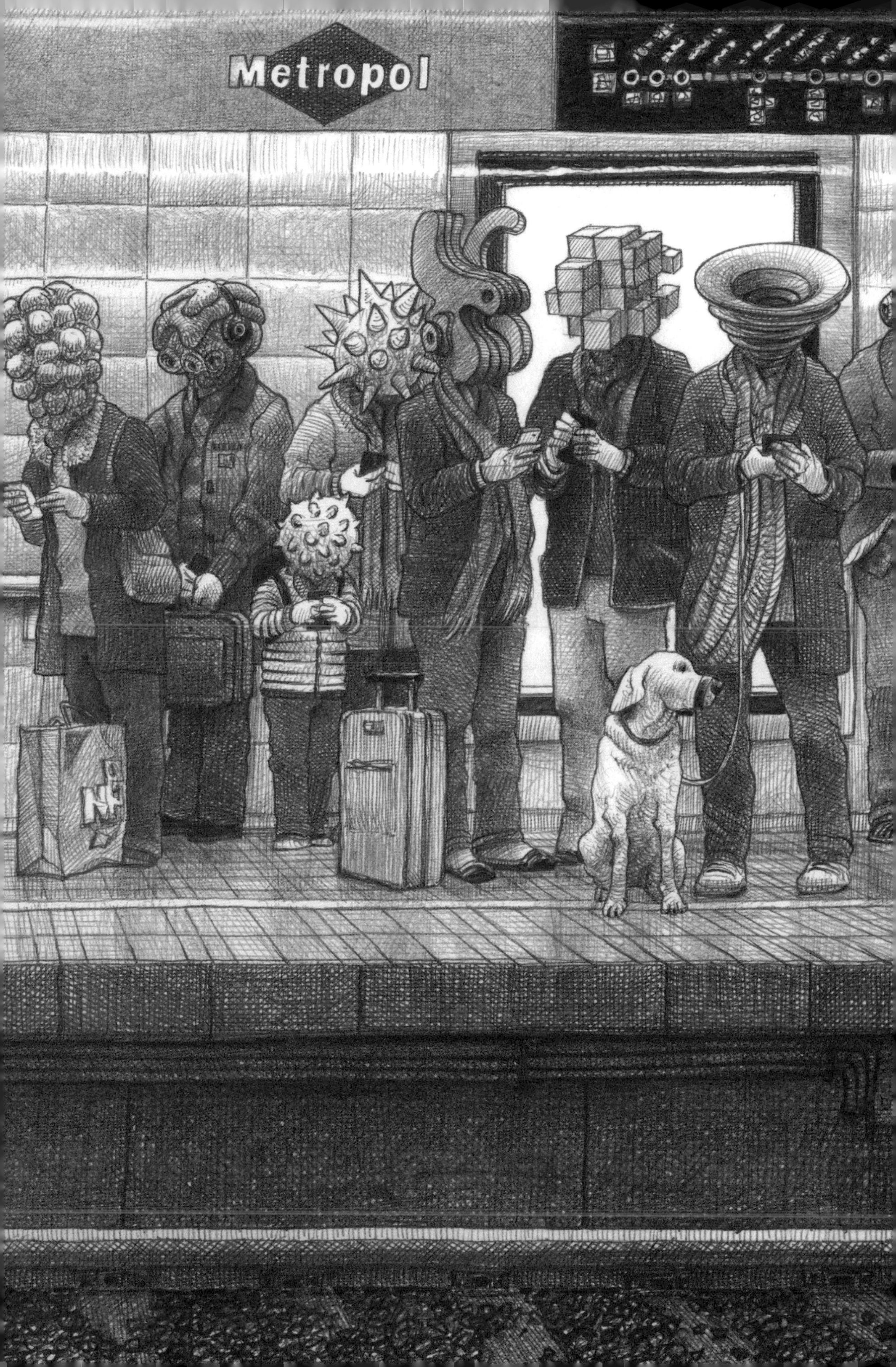
Metropol

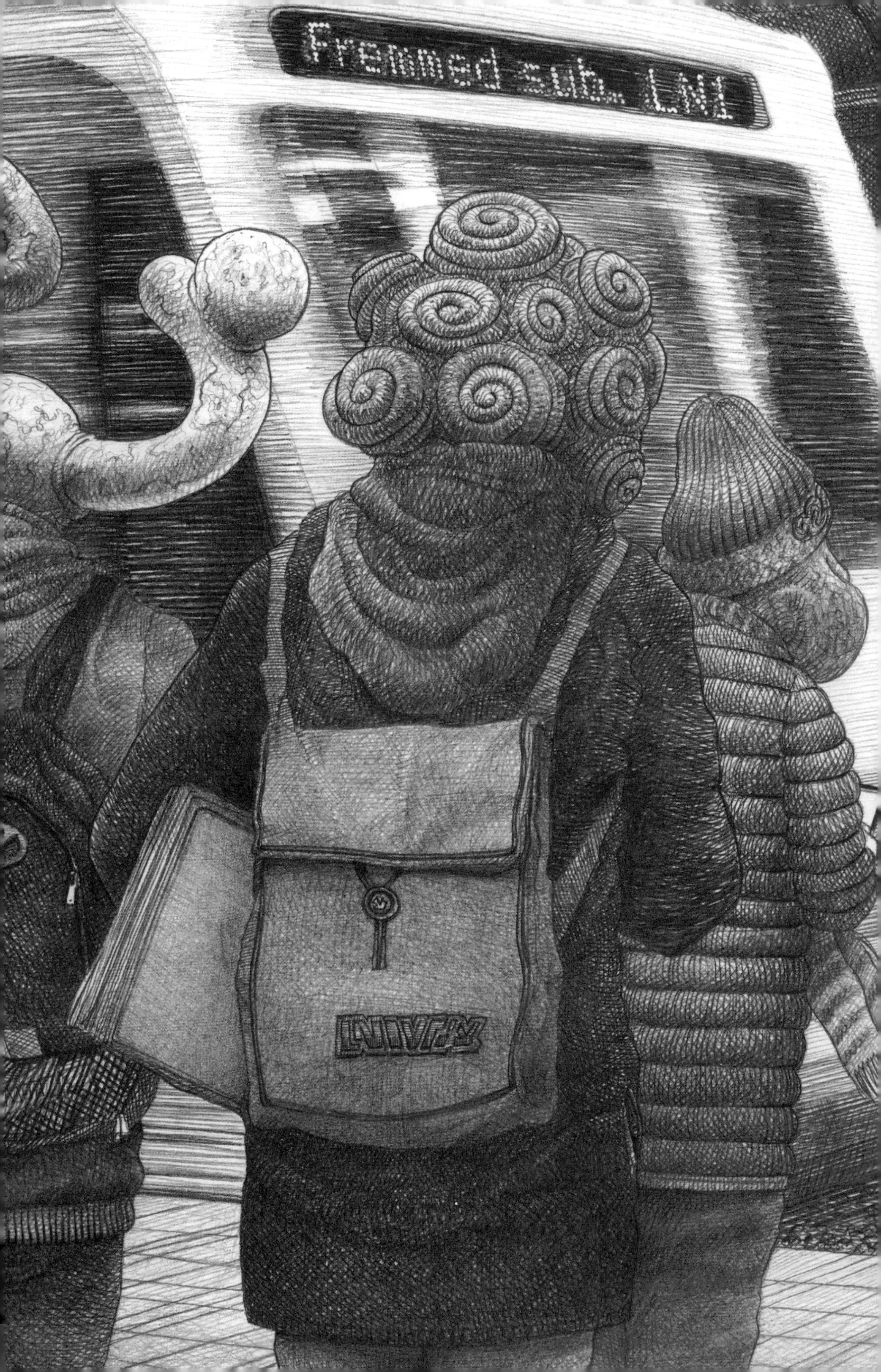
Fremmed sub. LN1

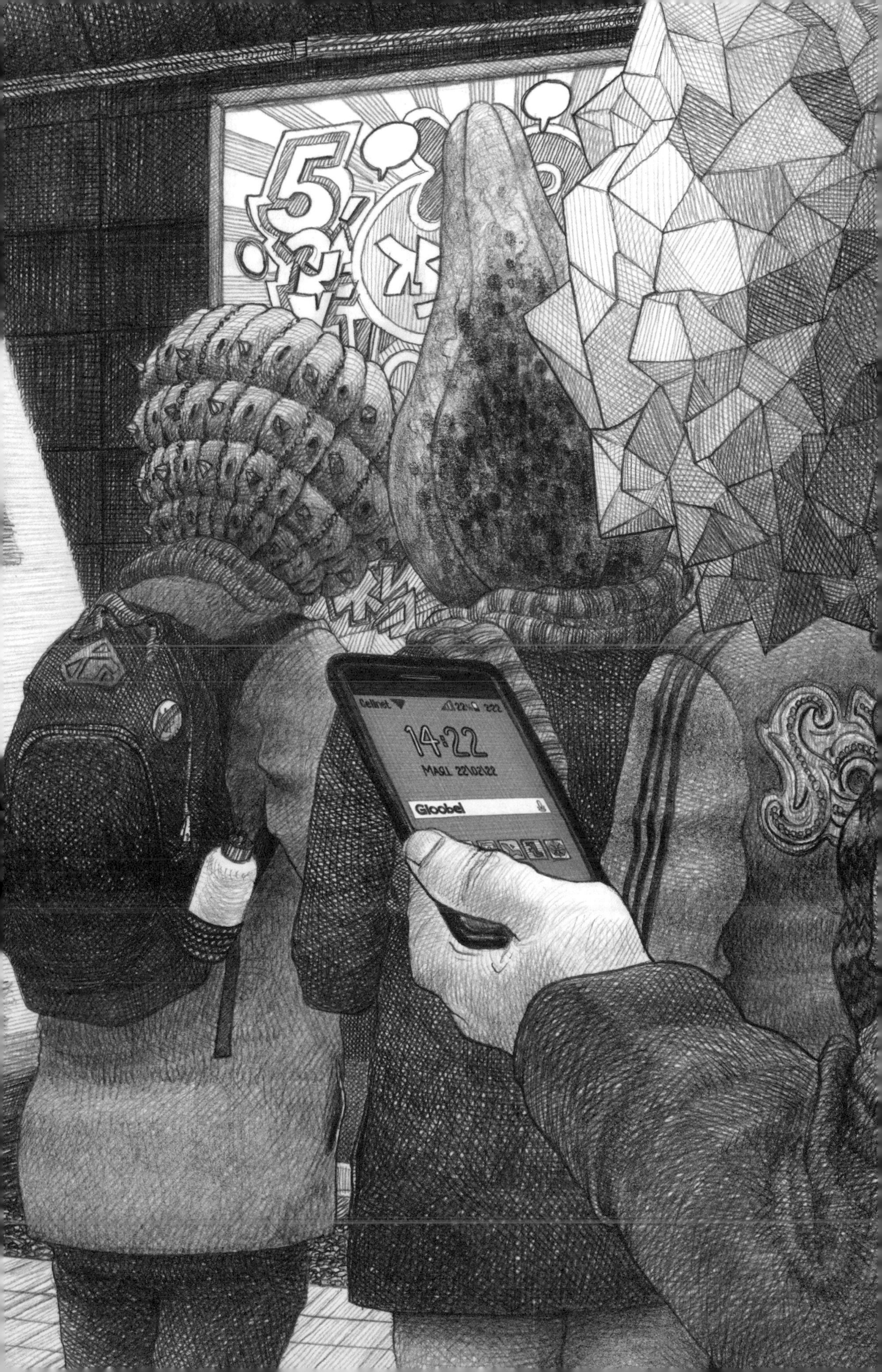

Cellnet
14:22
MAGL 22\02\22
Gloobel

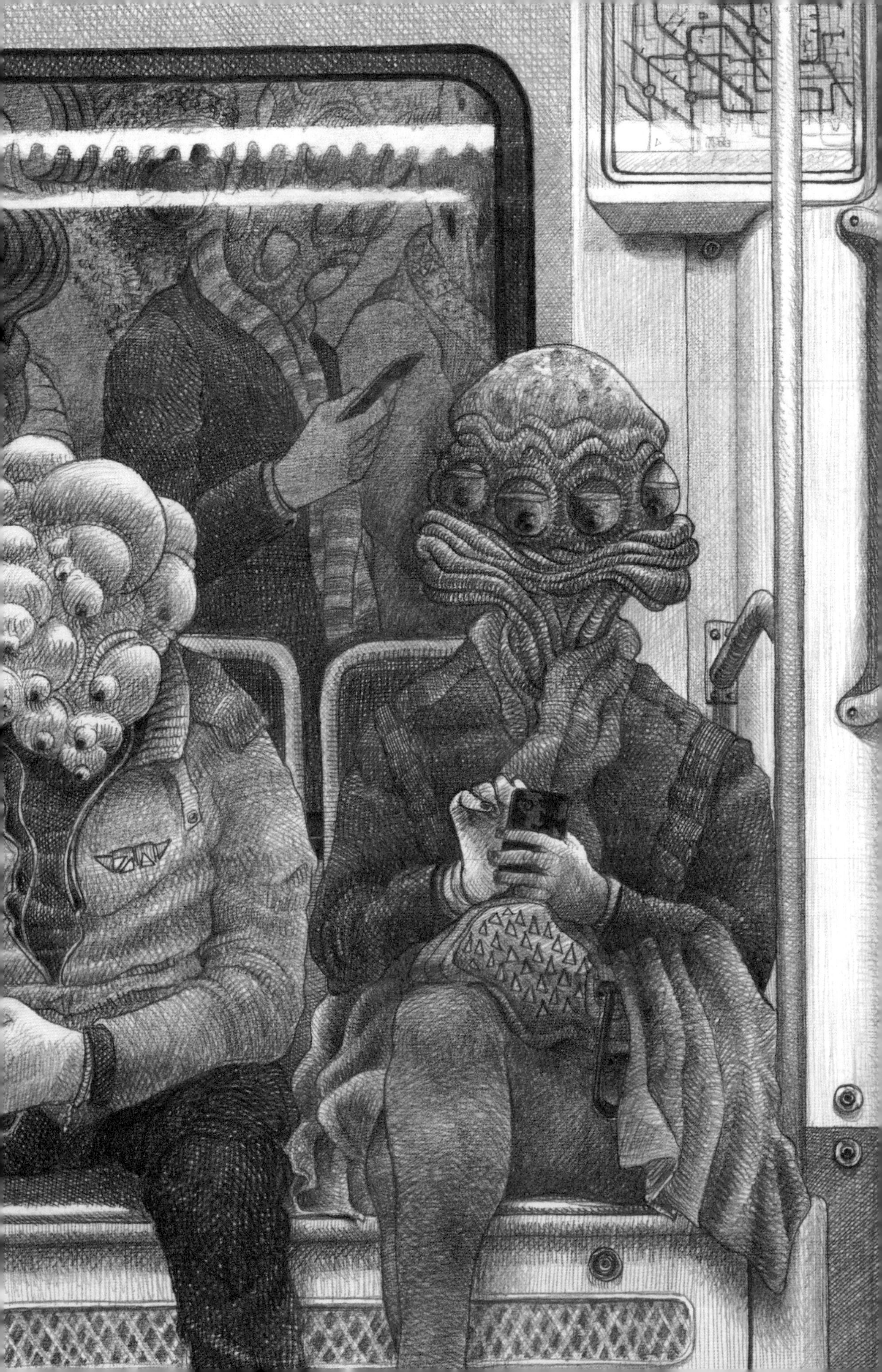

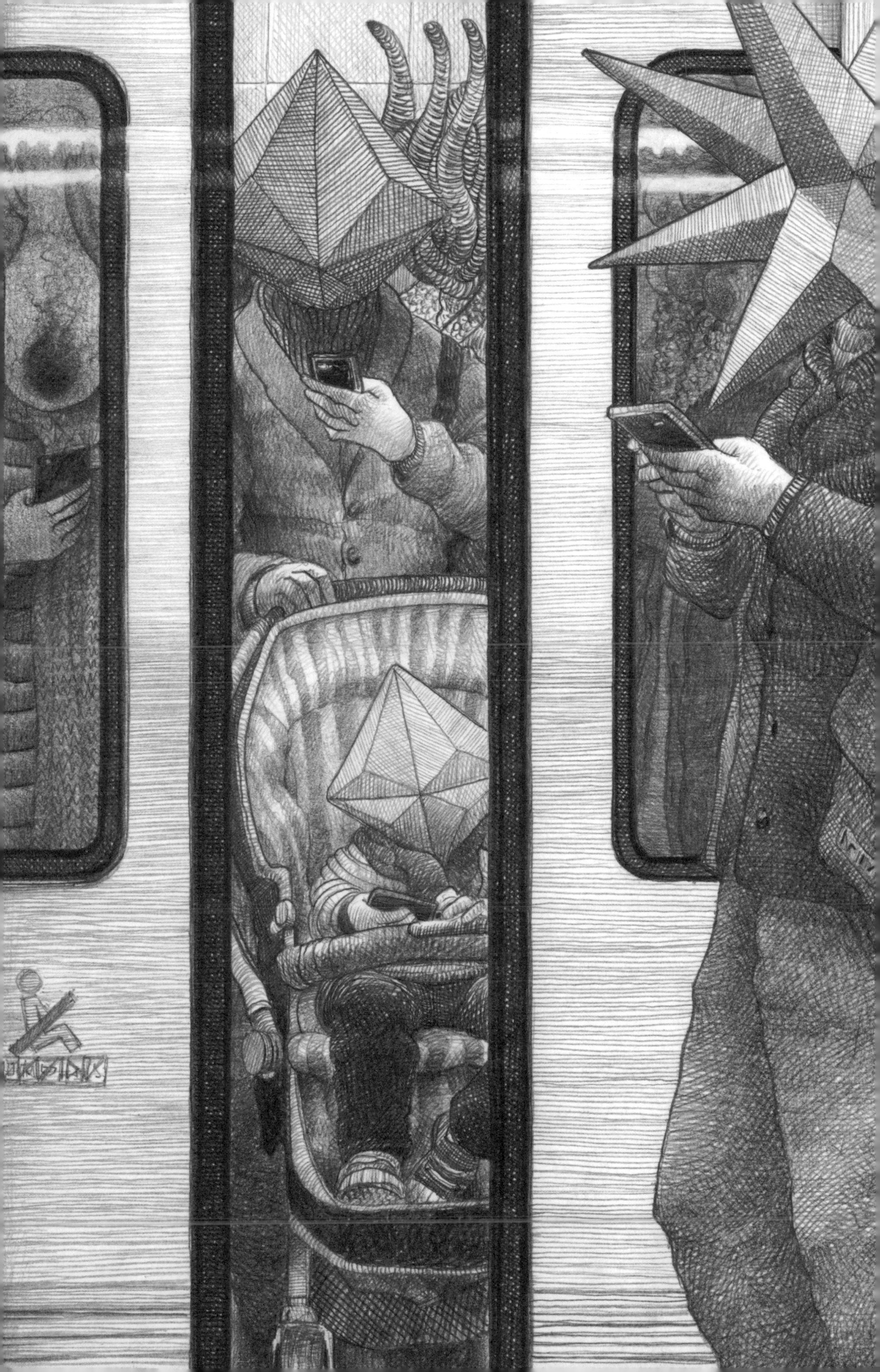

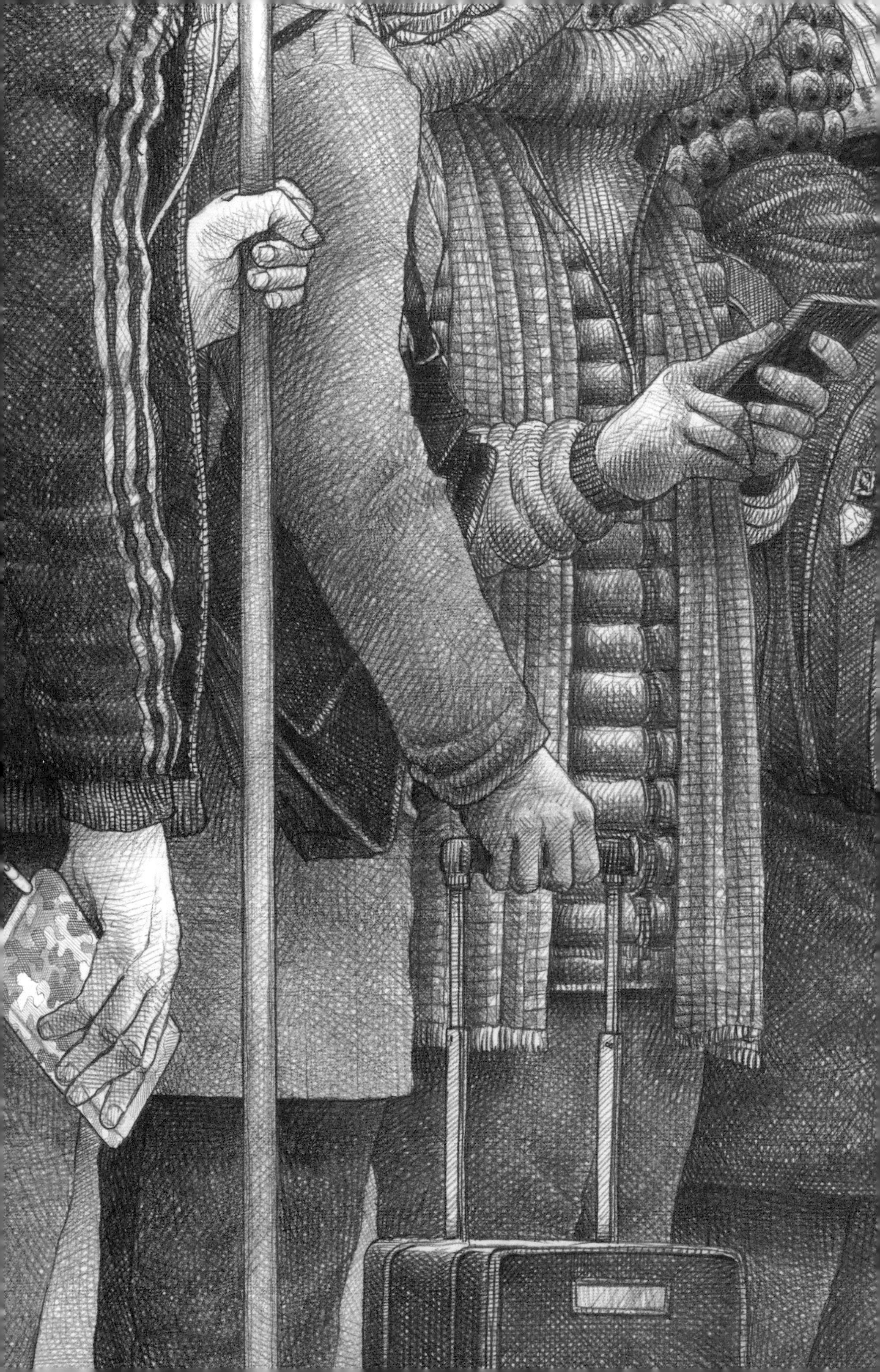

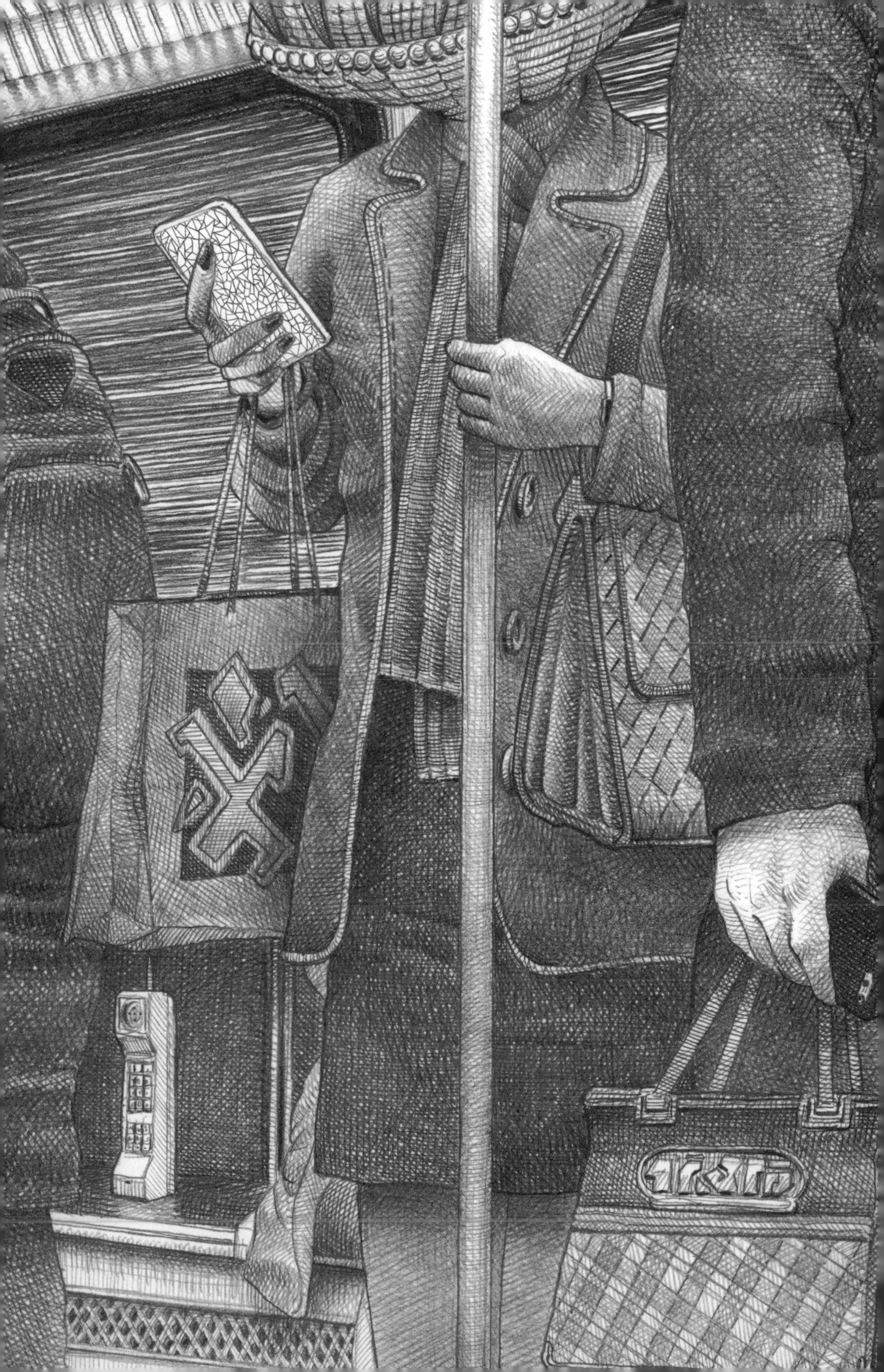

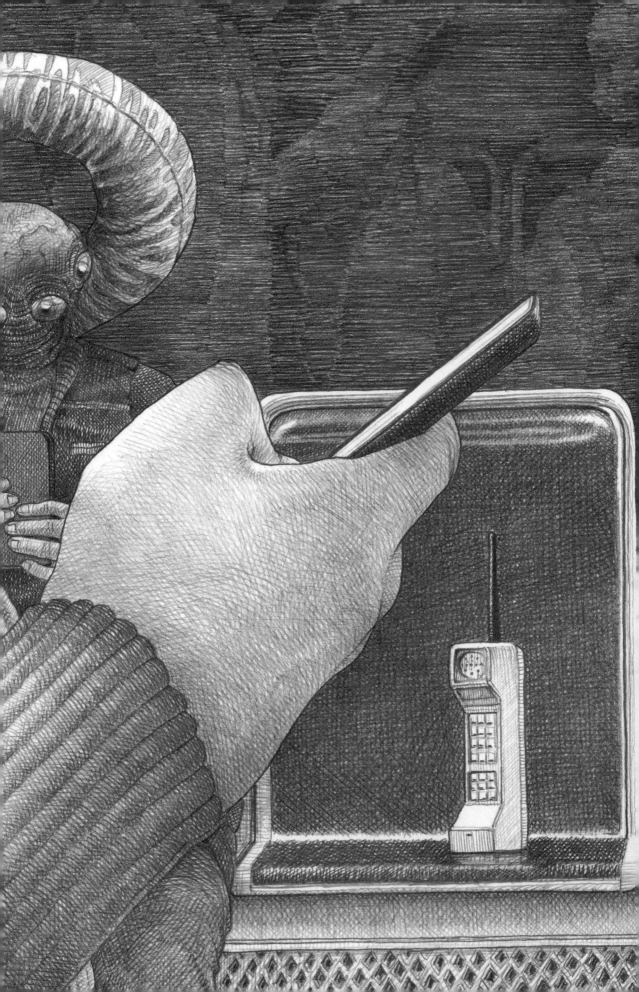

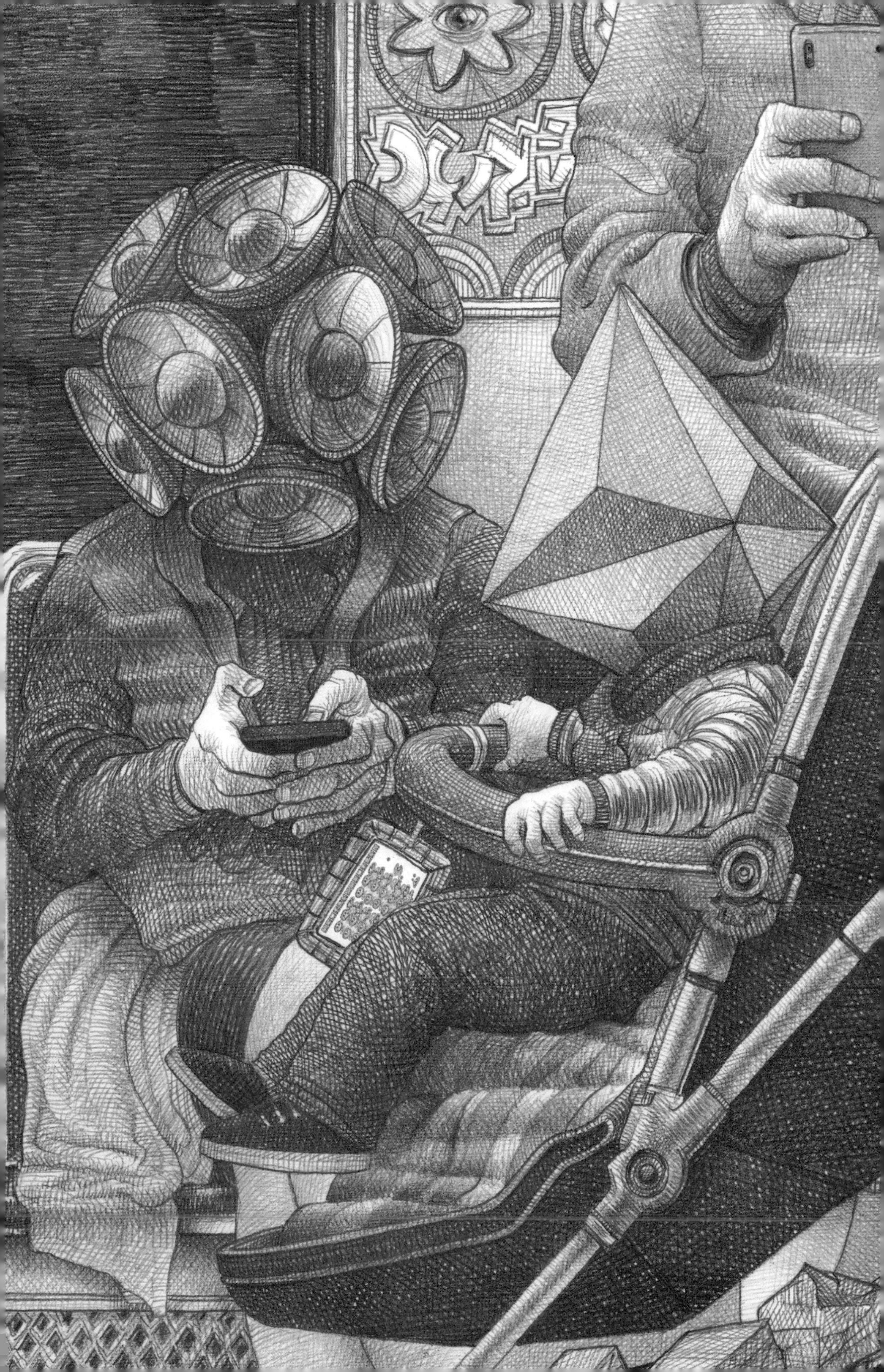

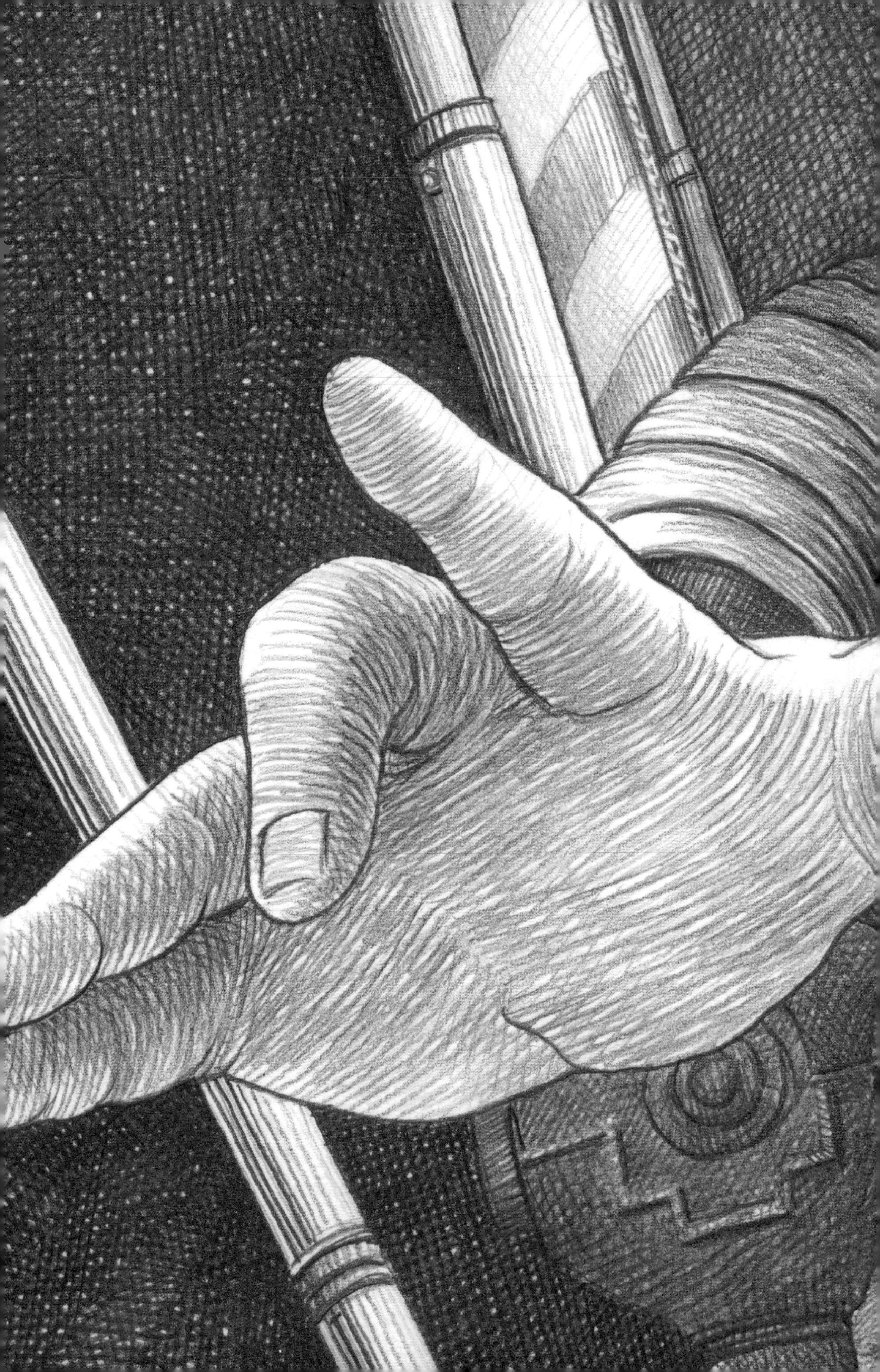

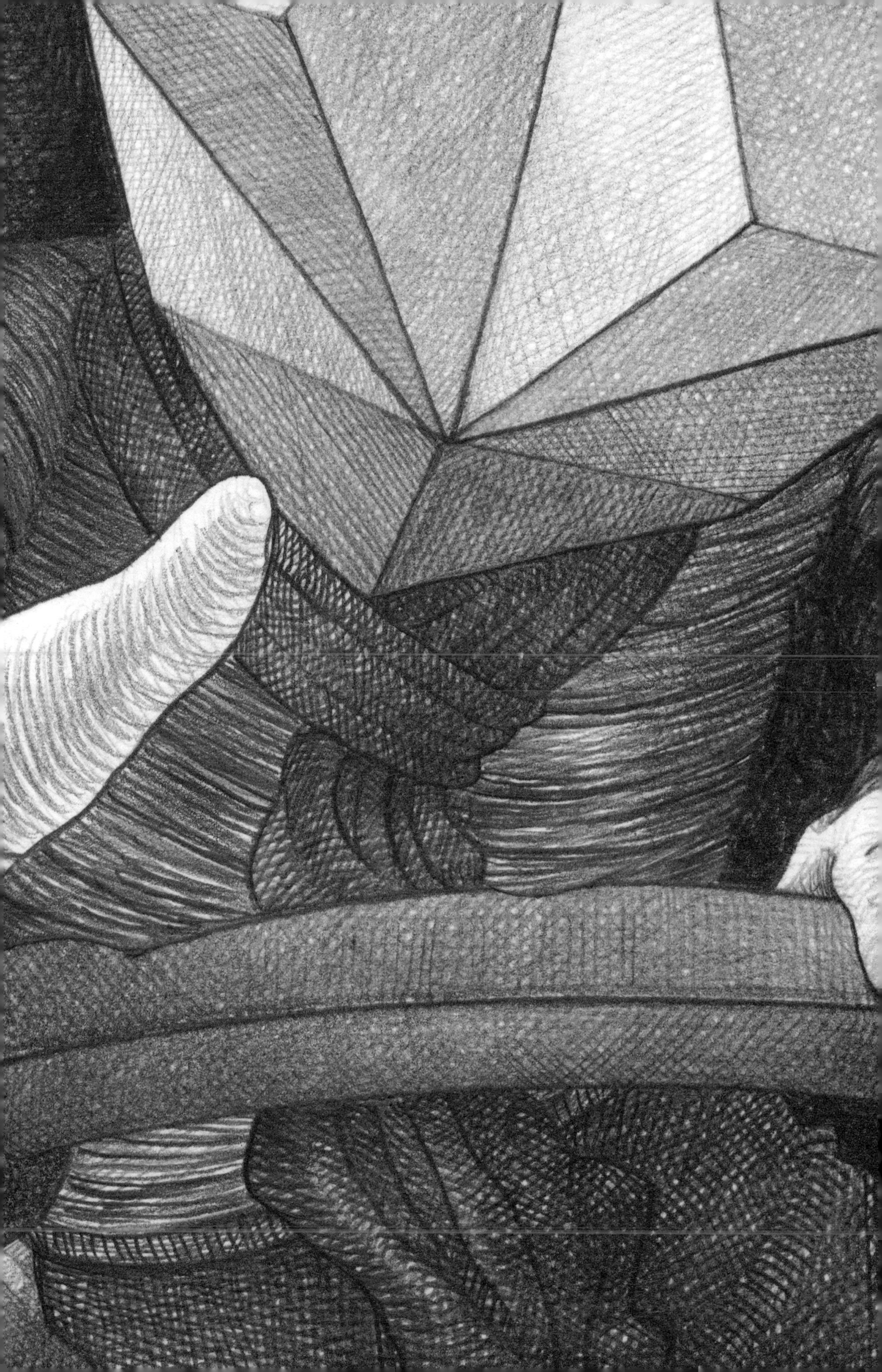

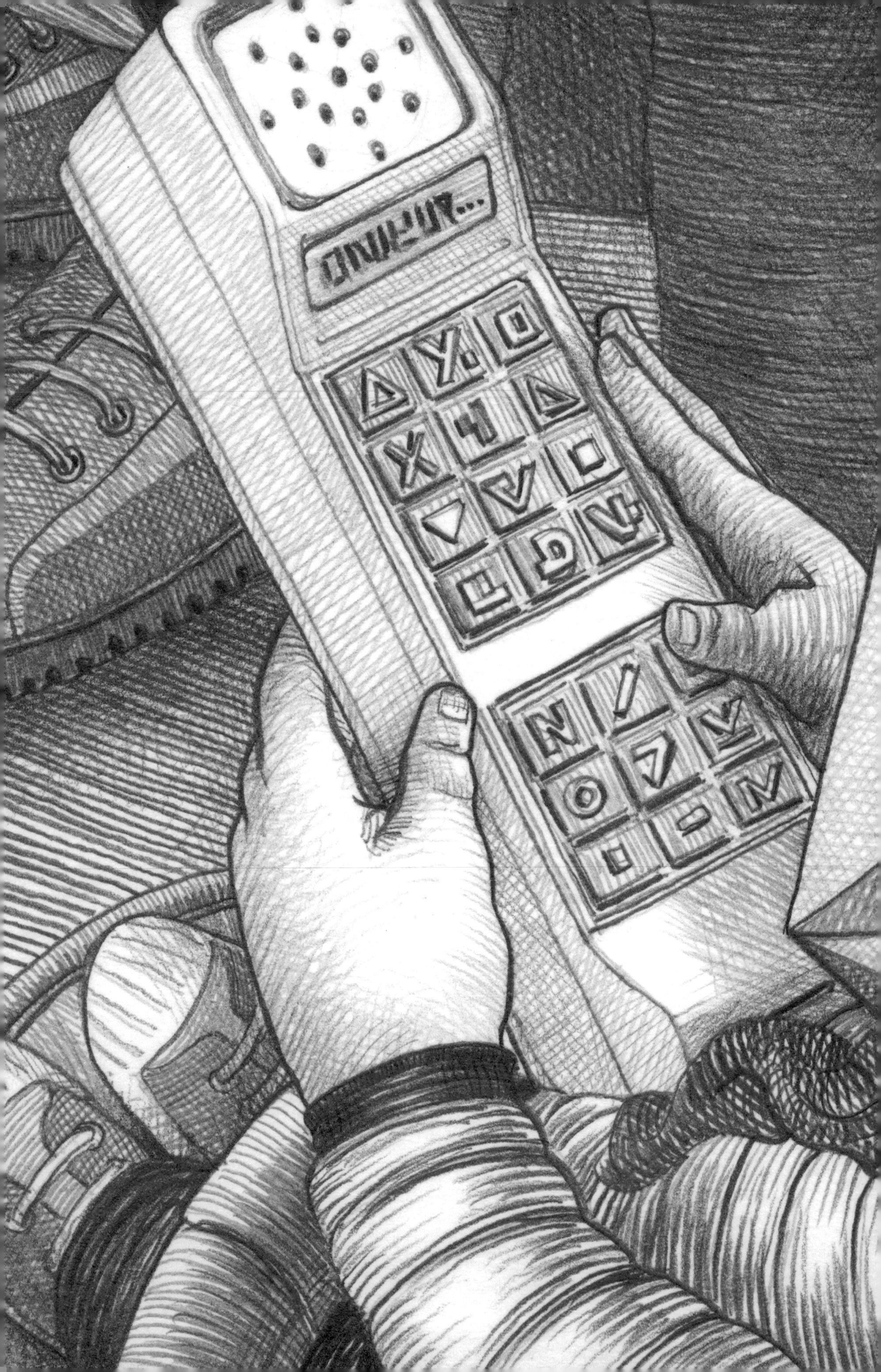

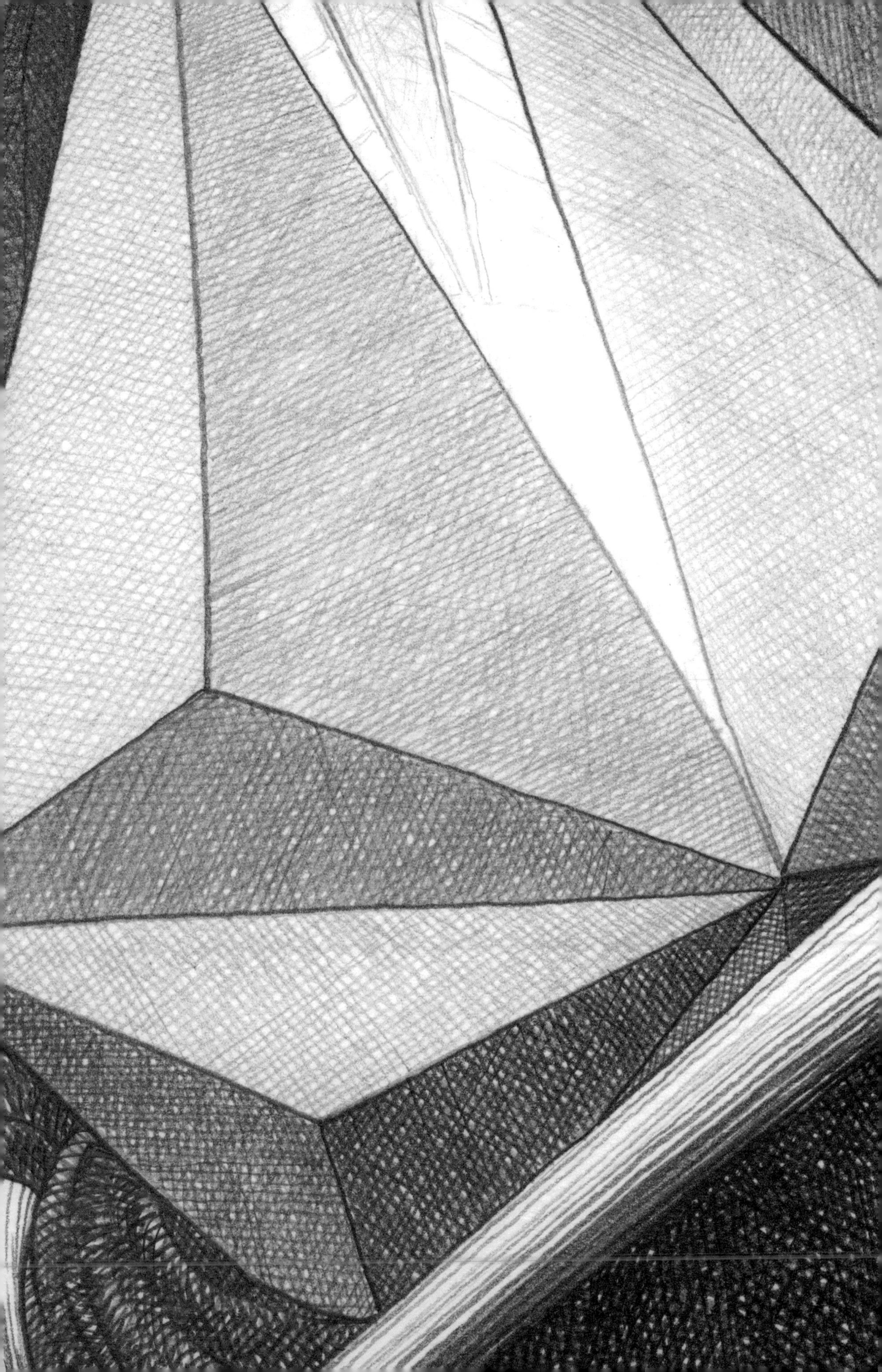

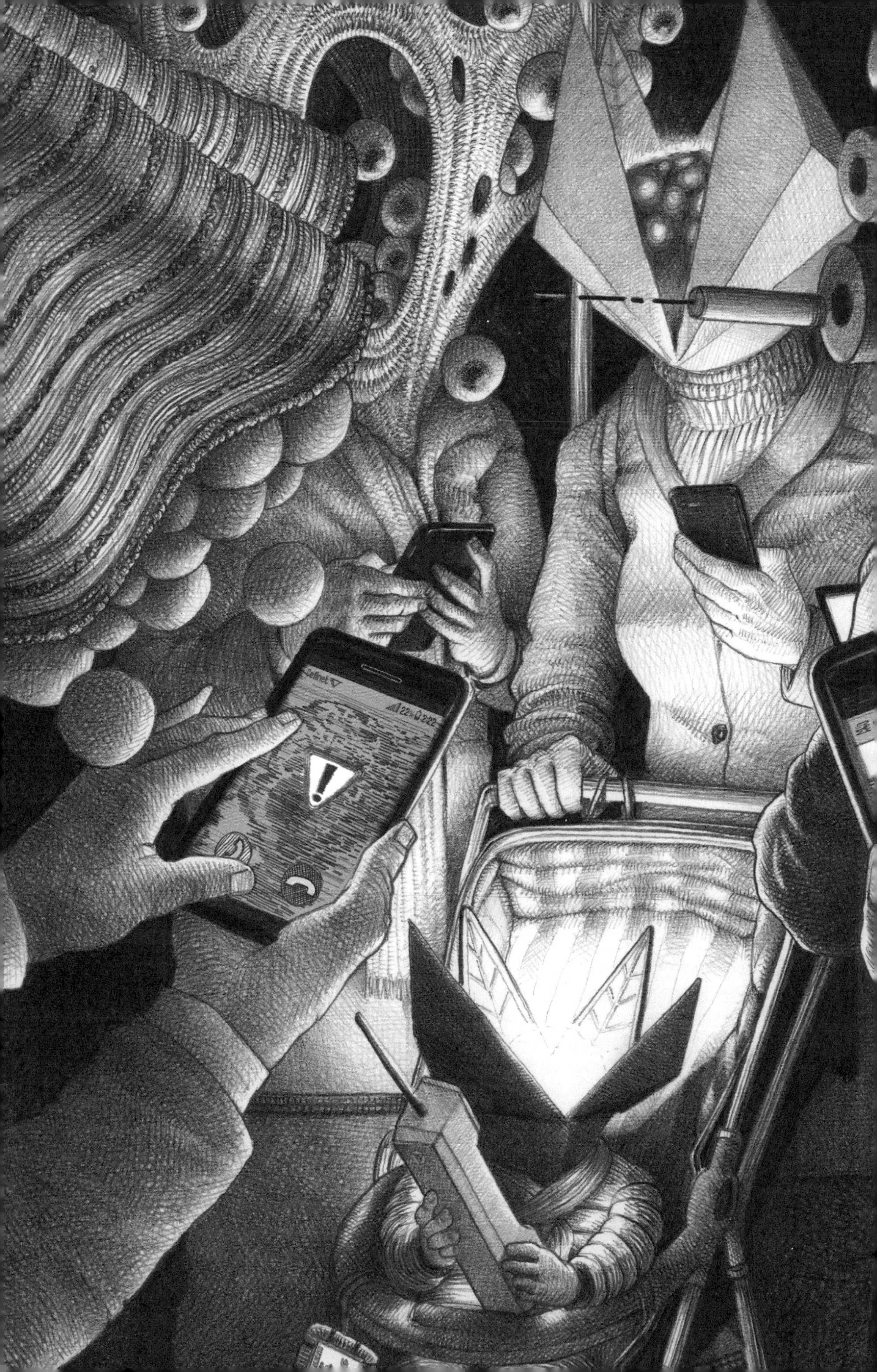
Cellnet
22 2:22

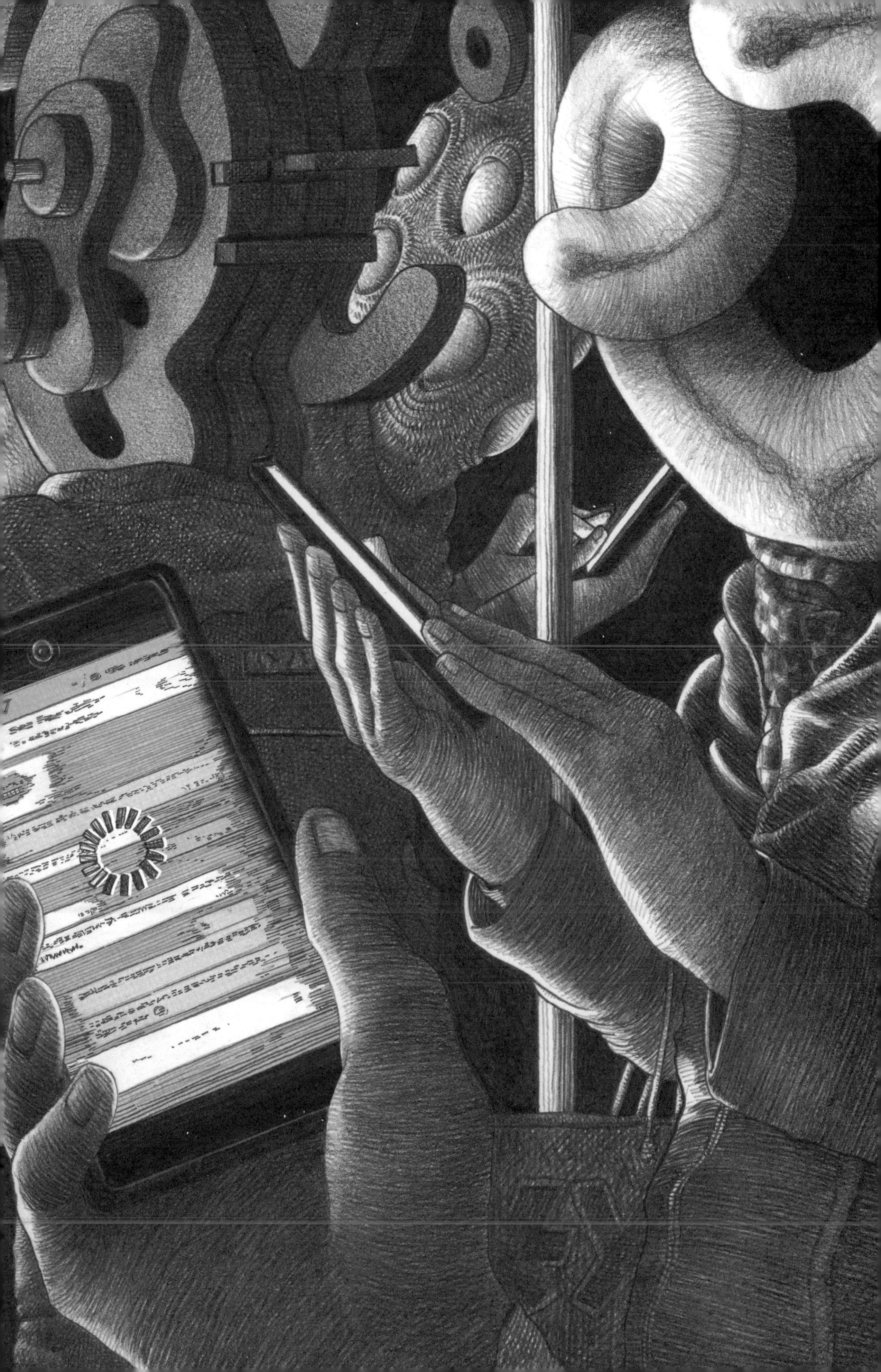

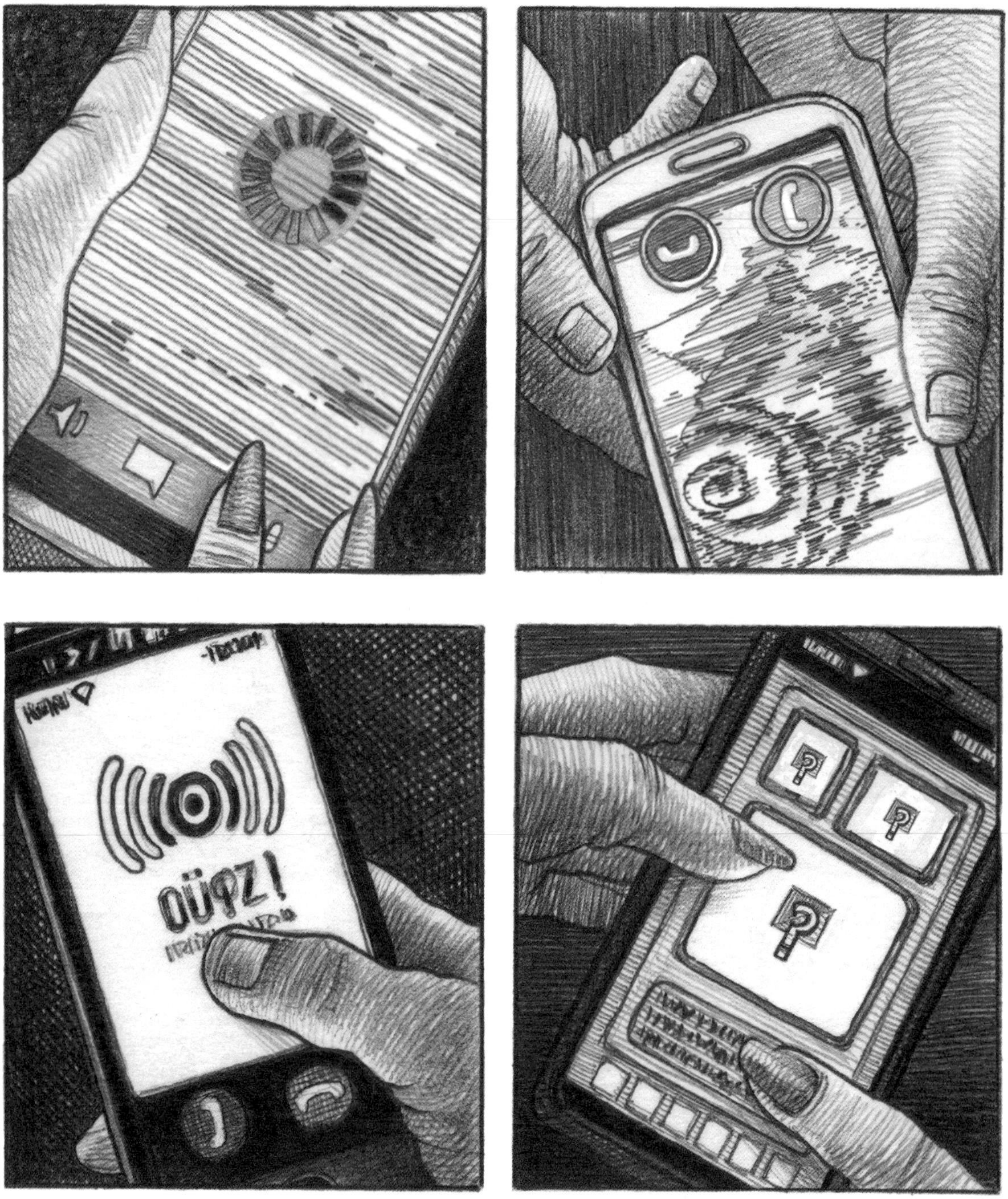
OÜPZ!

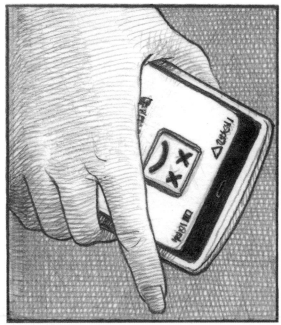

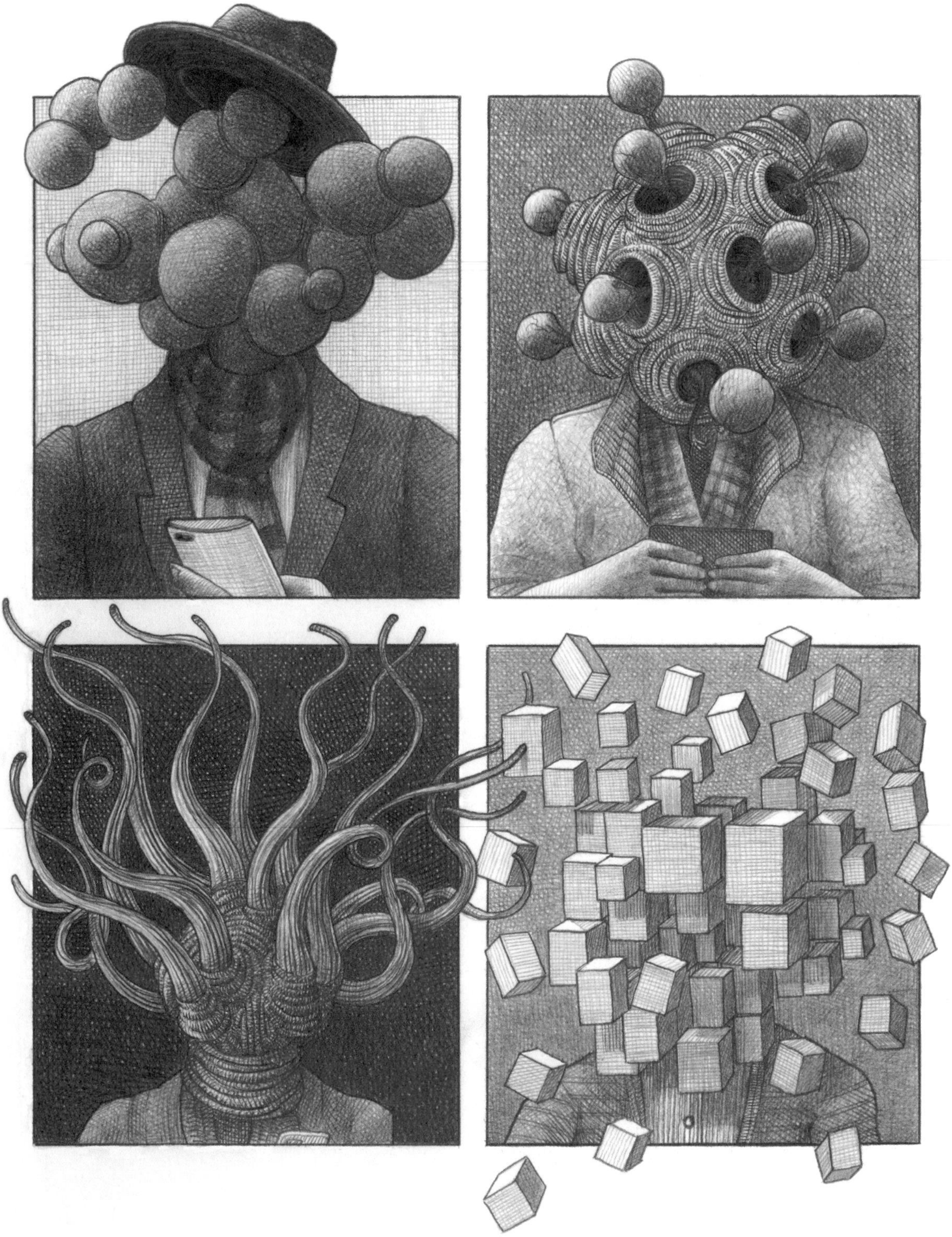

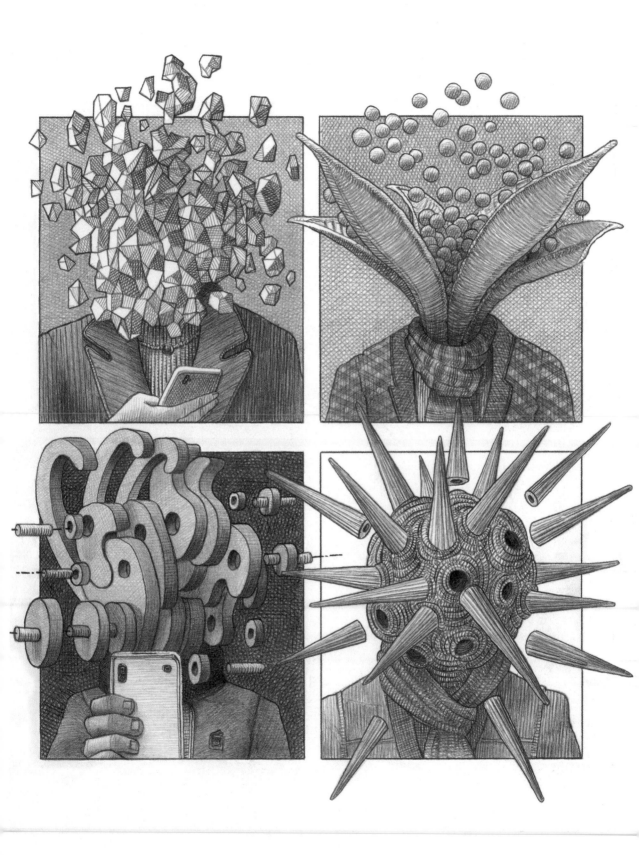

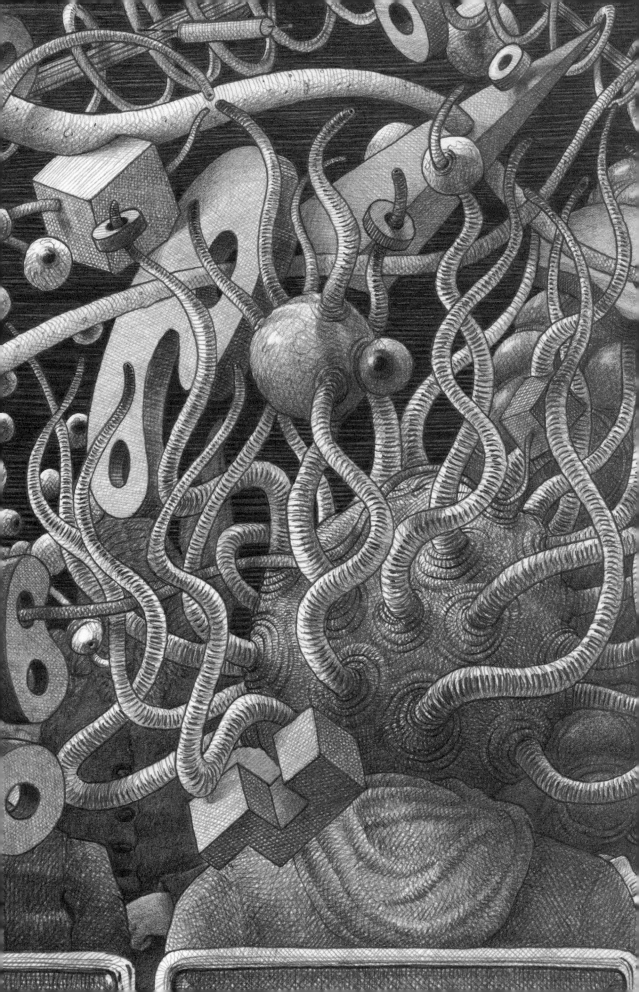

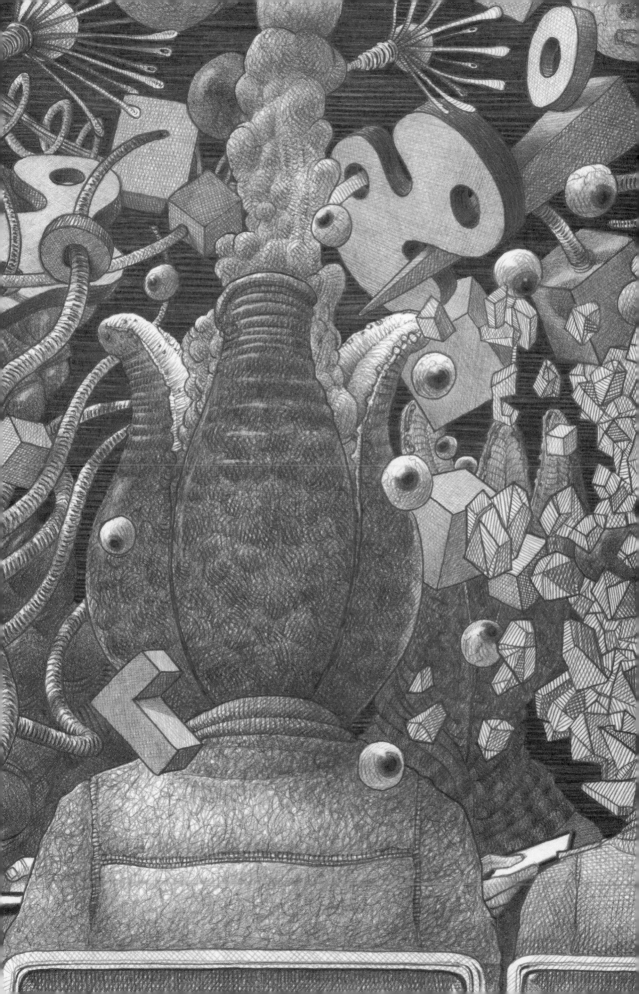

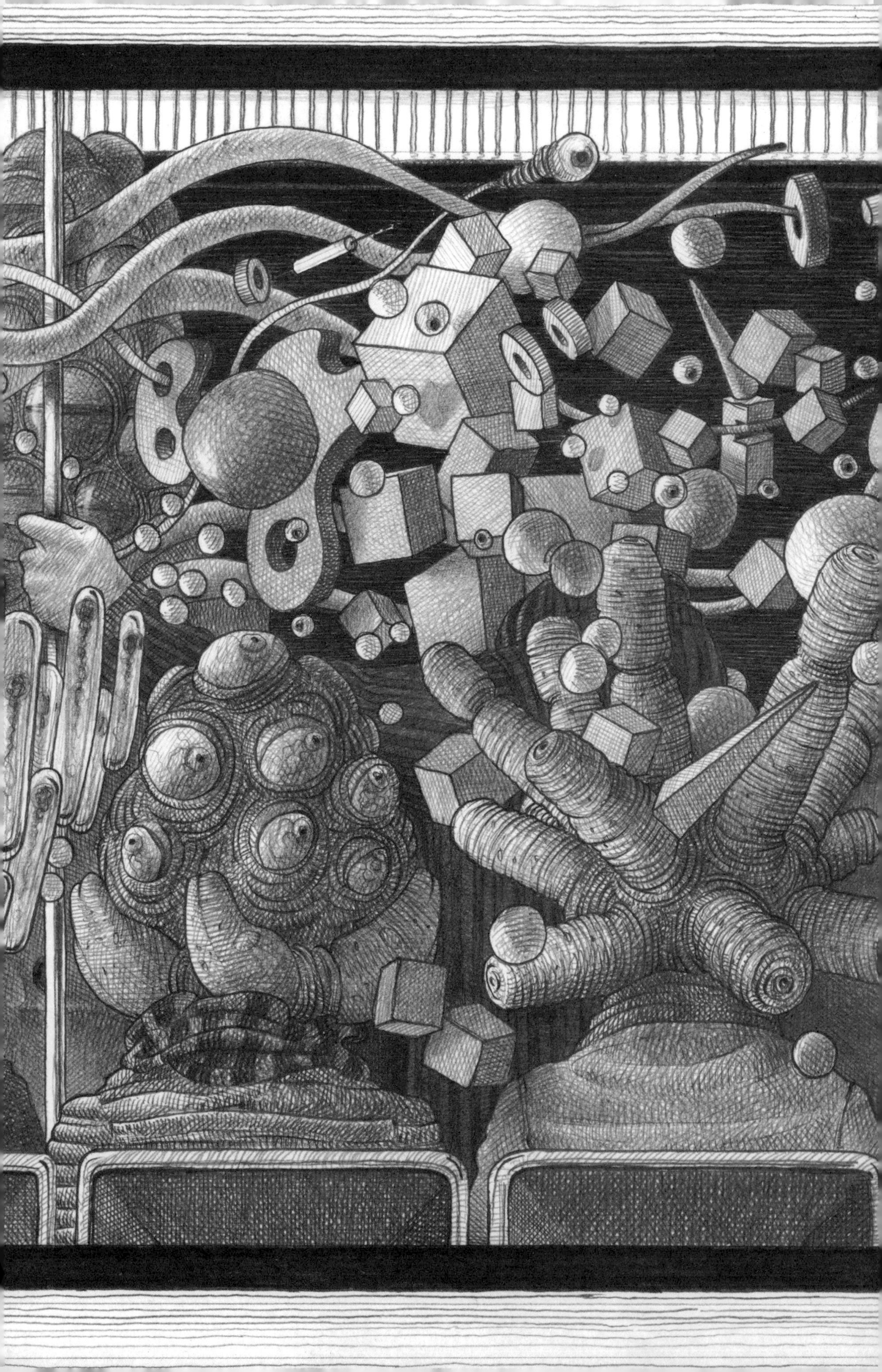

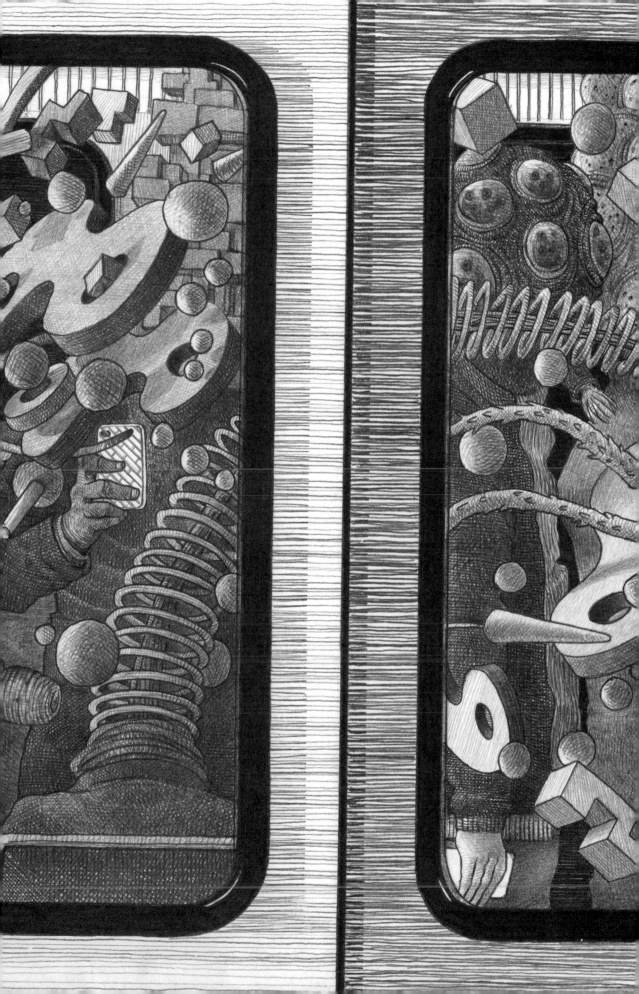

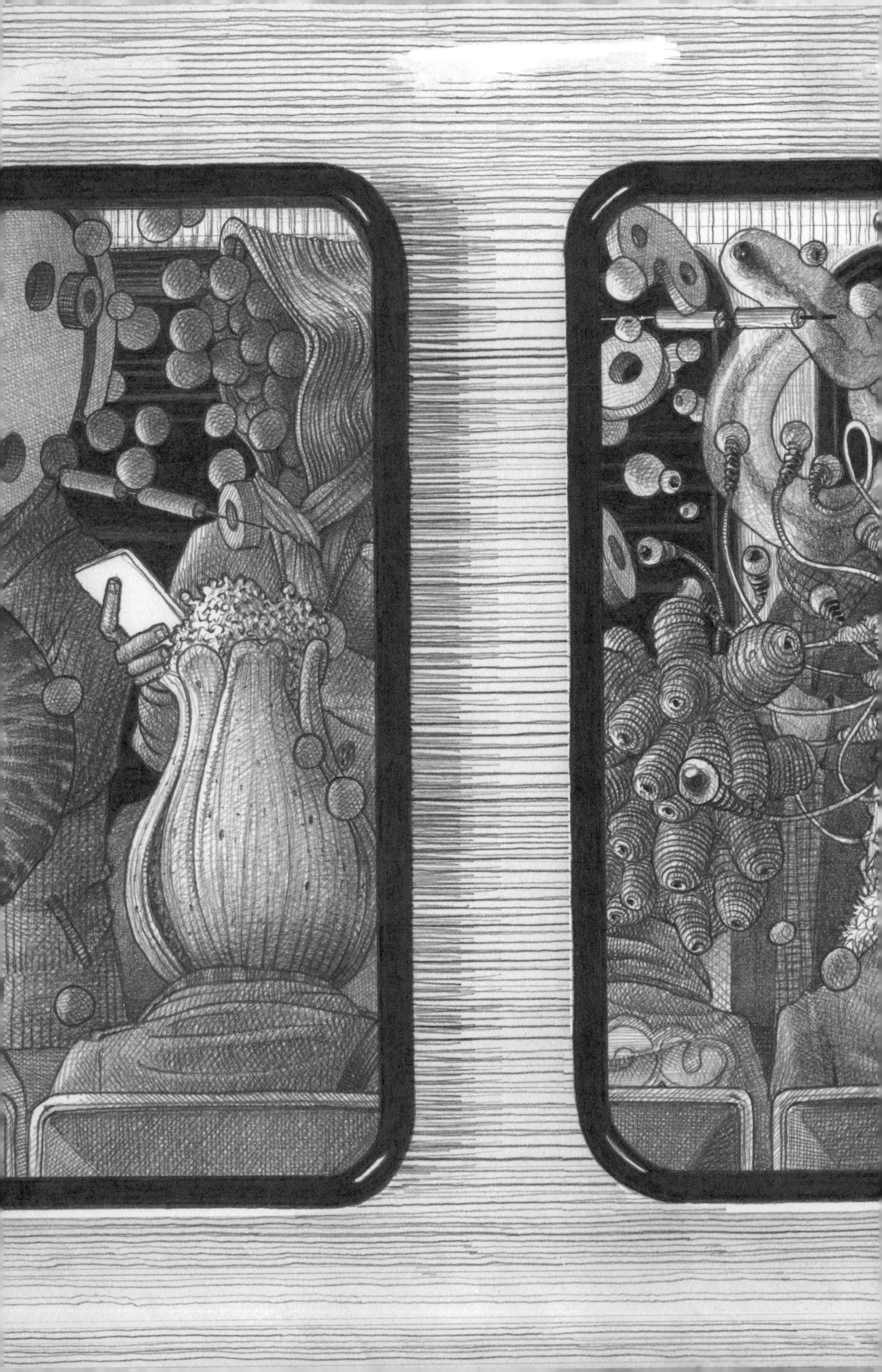

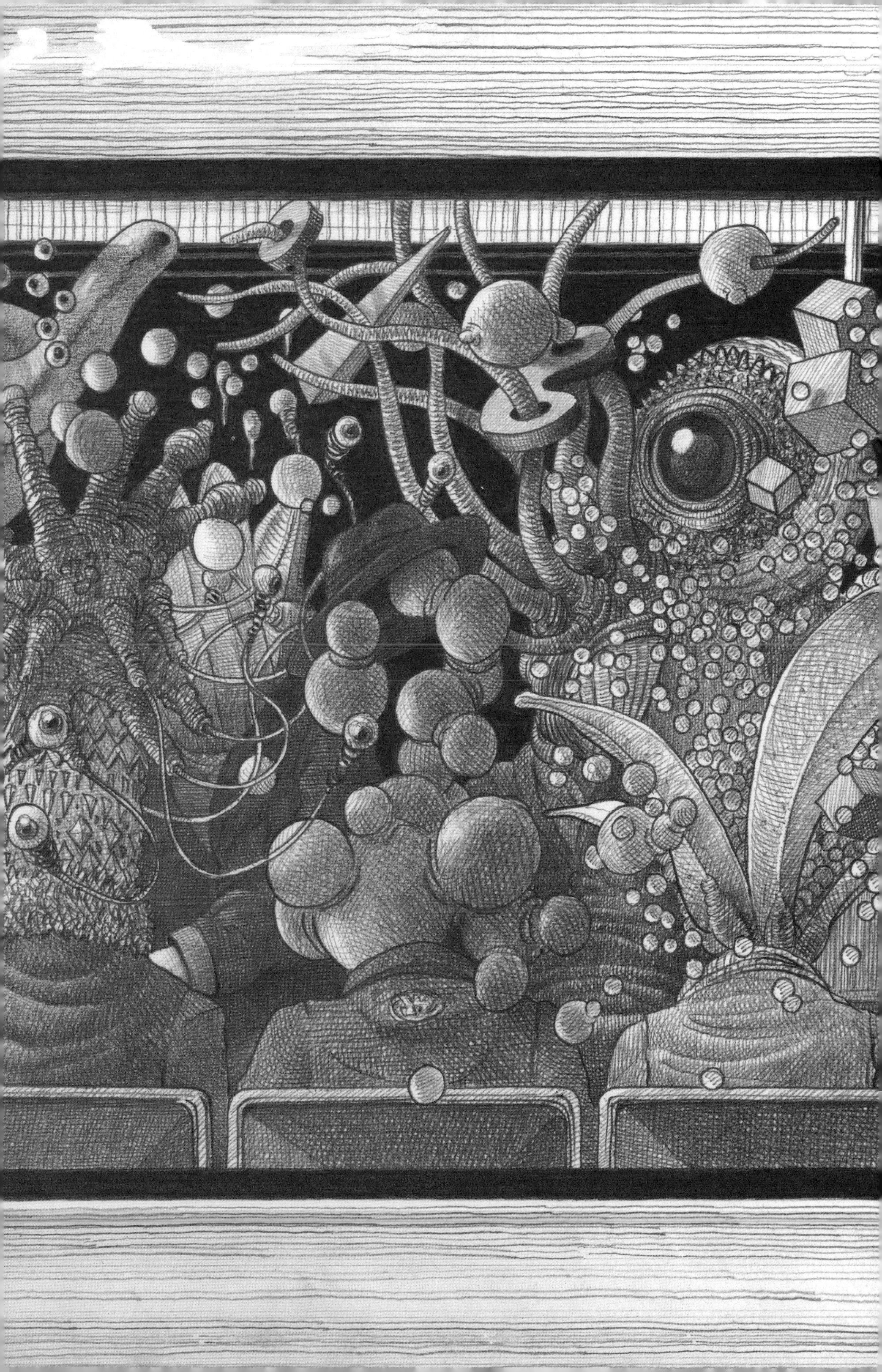

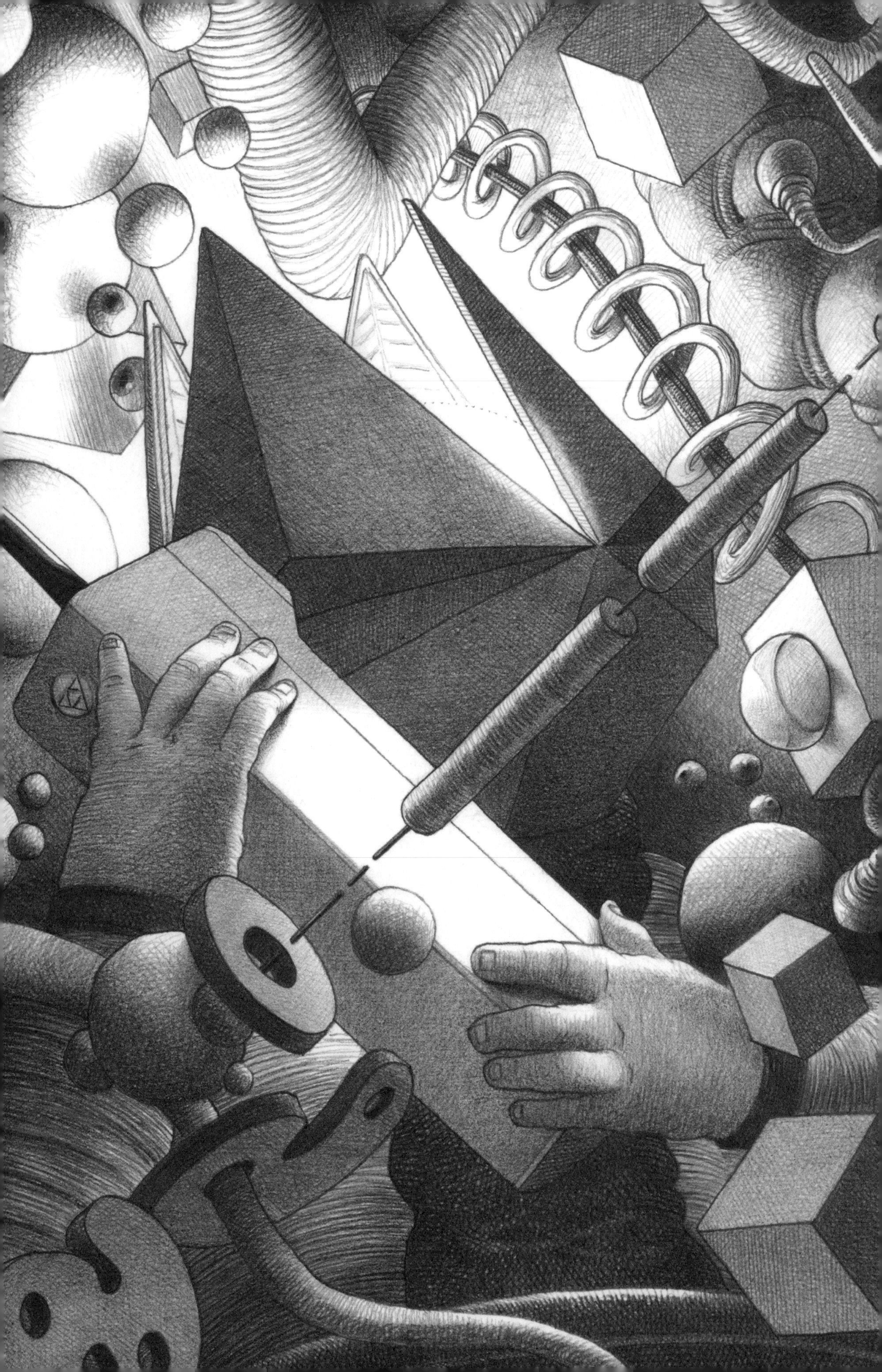

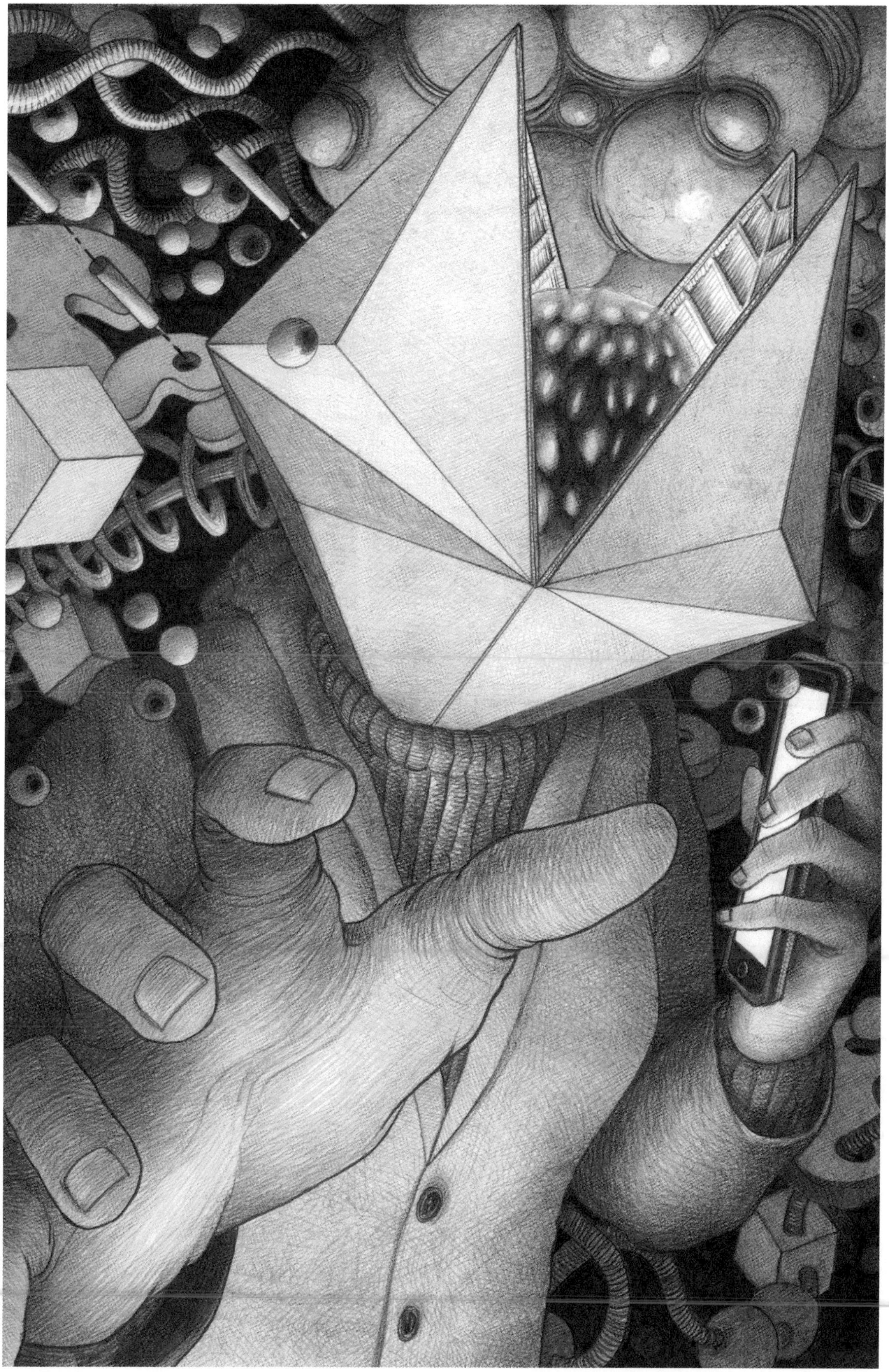

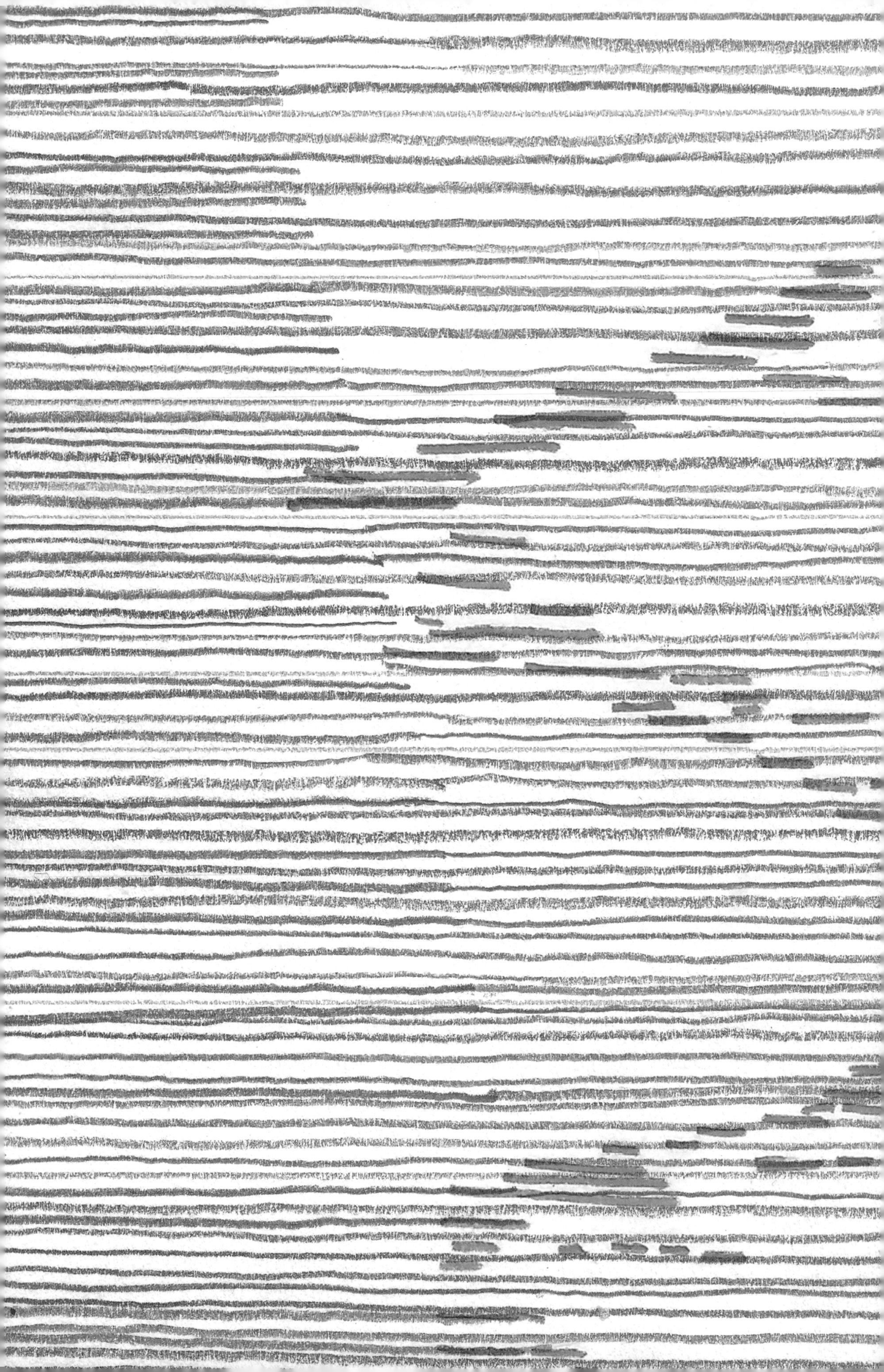

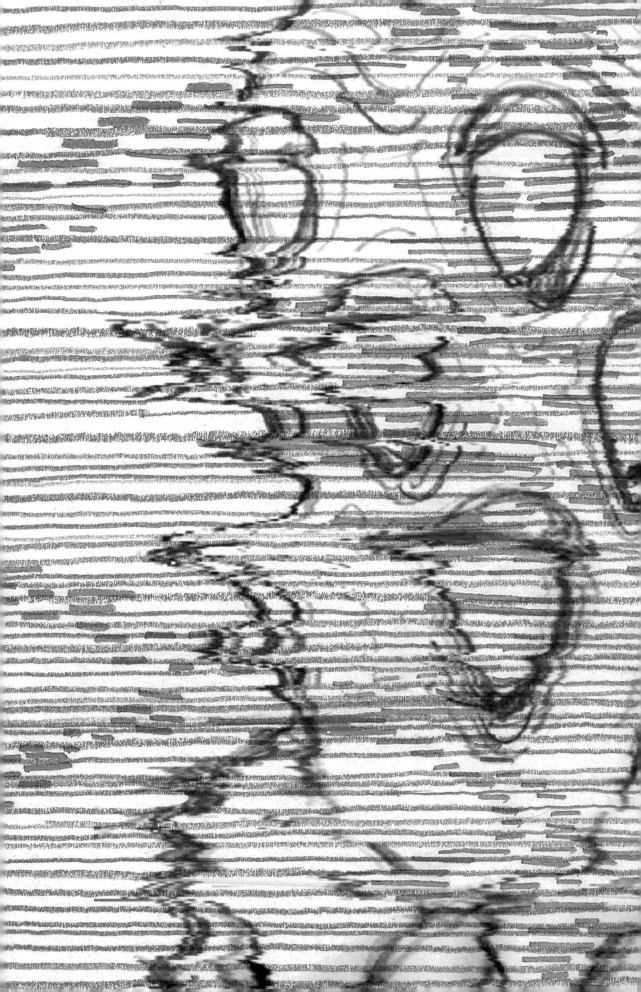

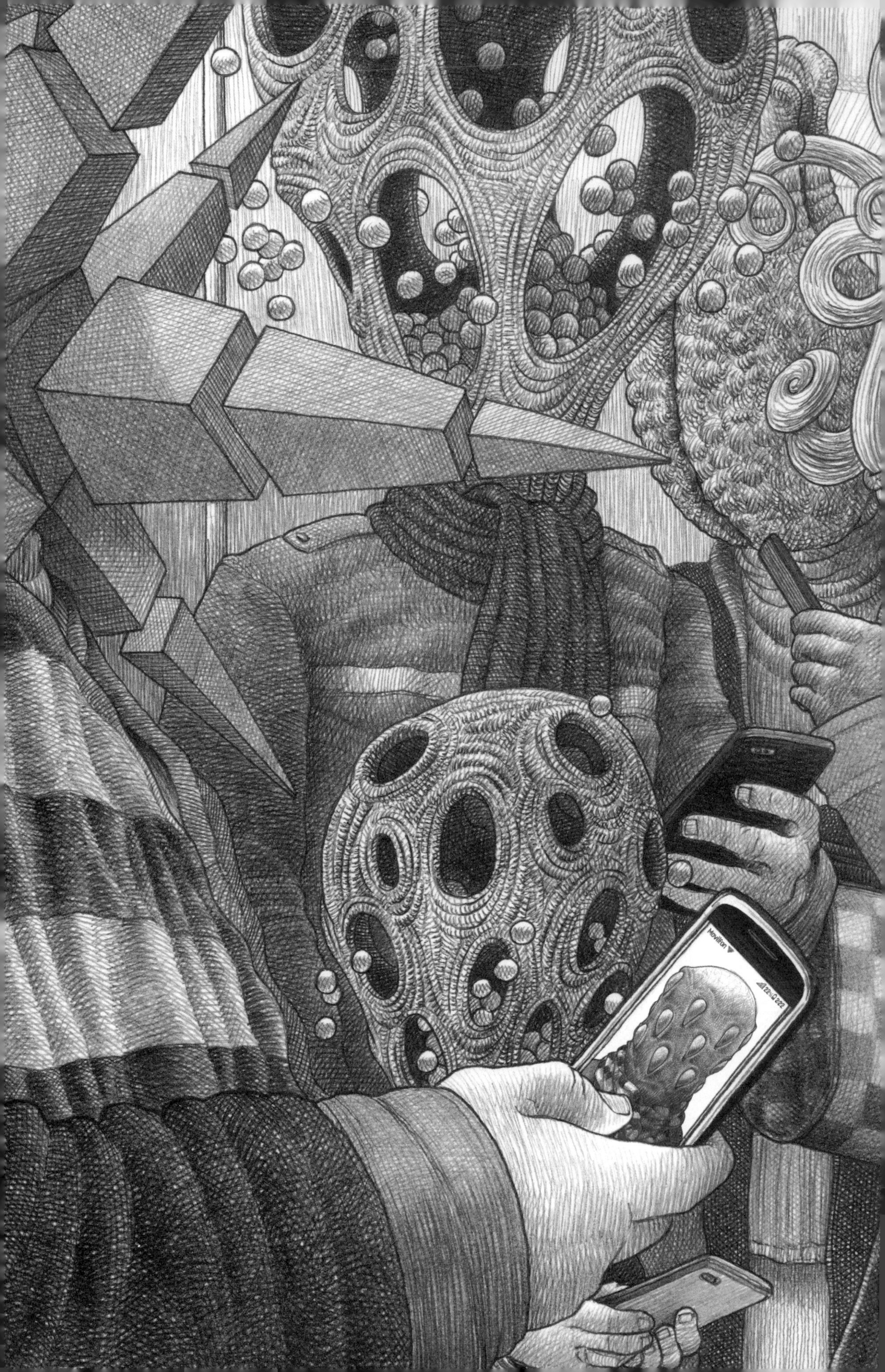
Movilfon

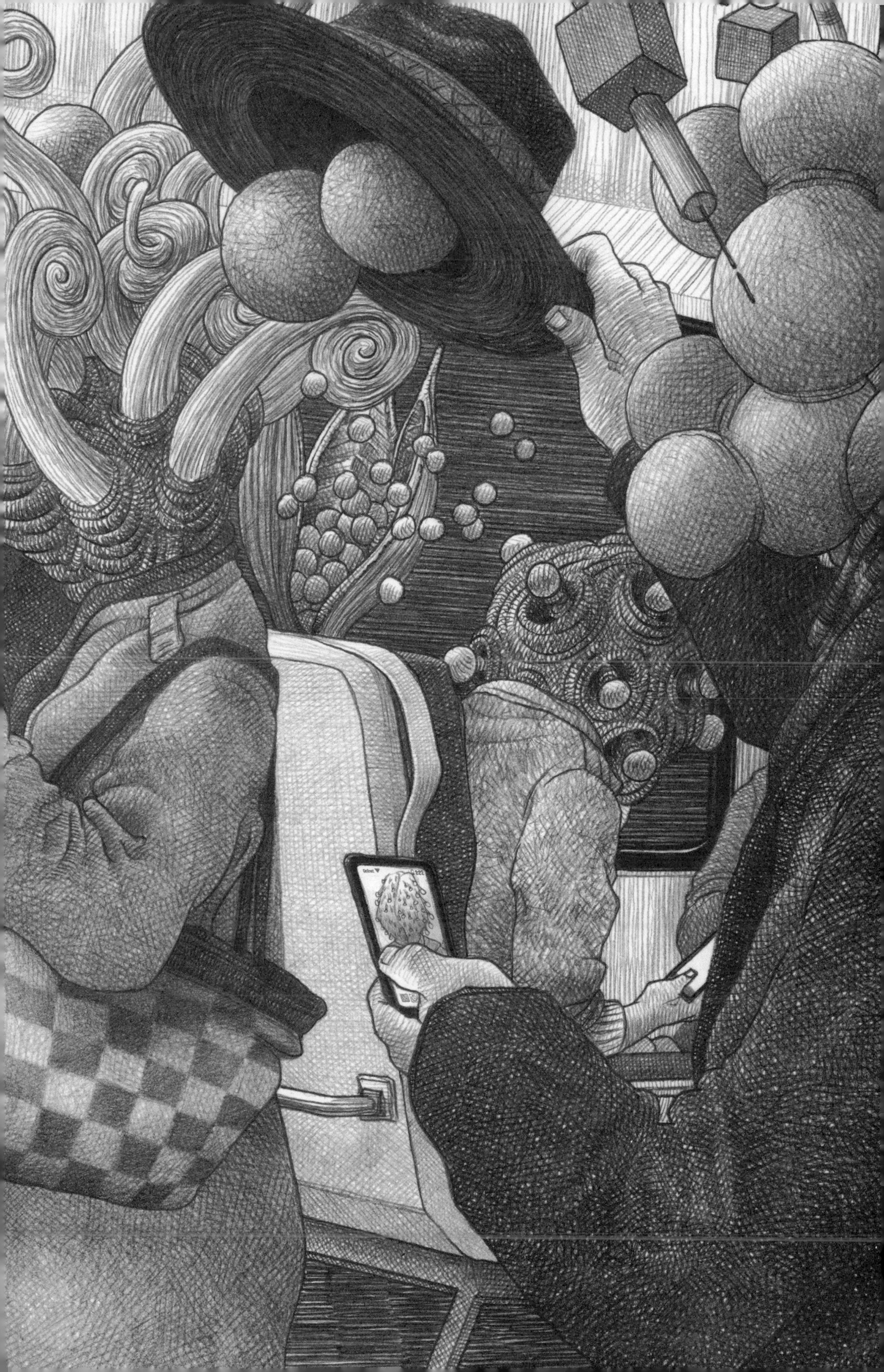

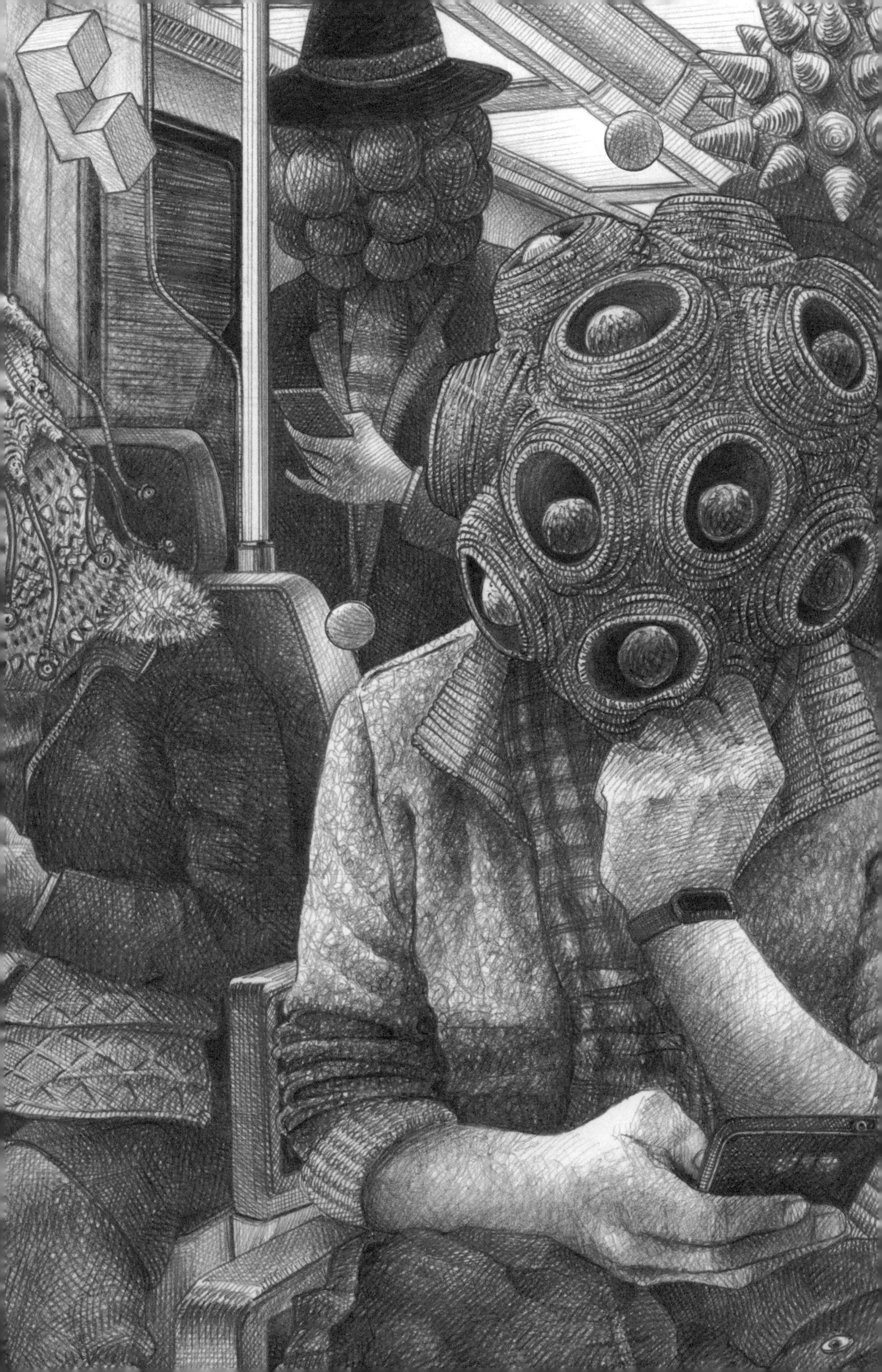

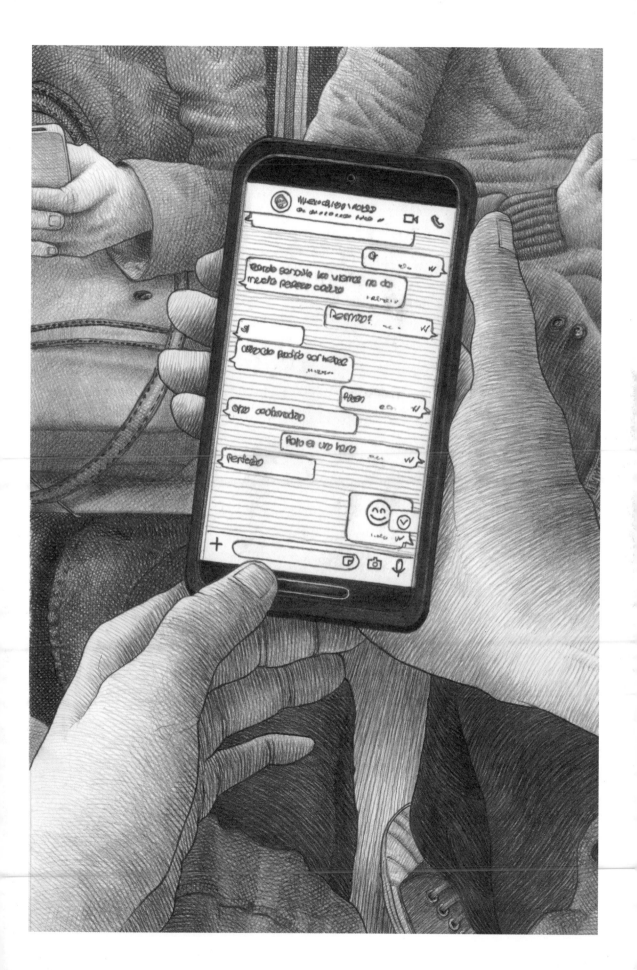

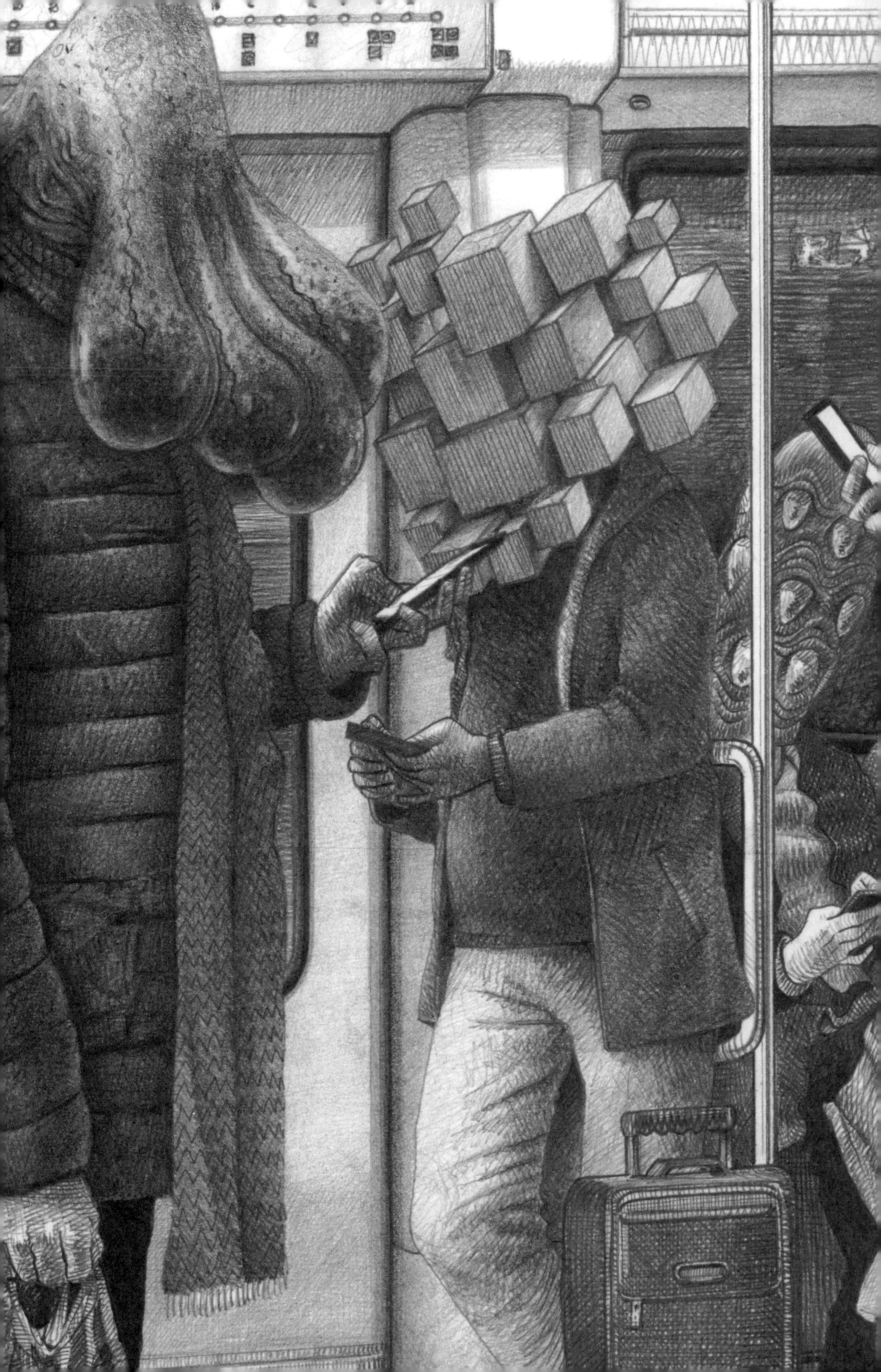

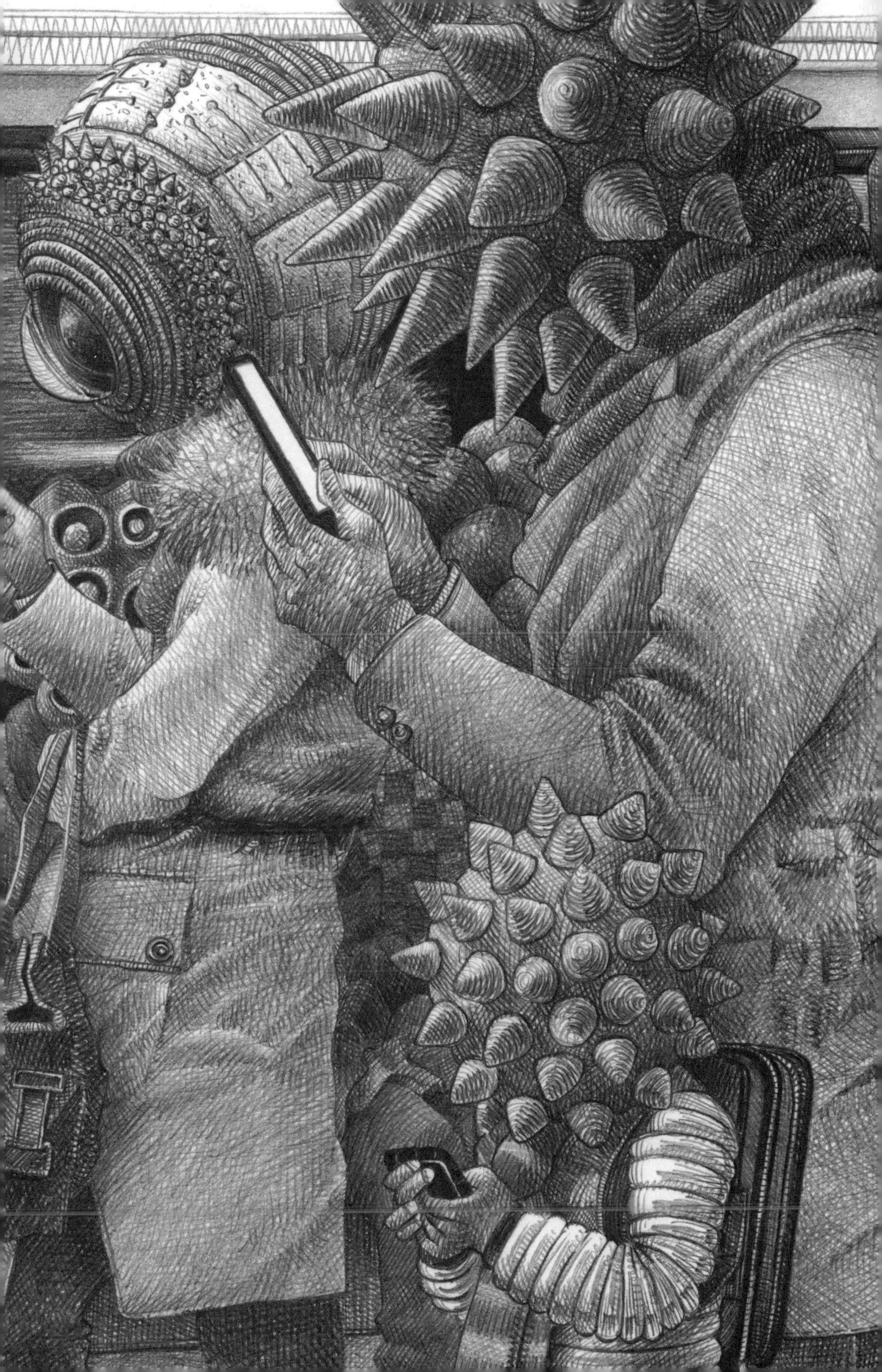

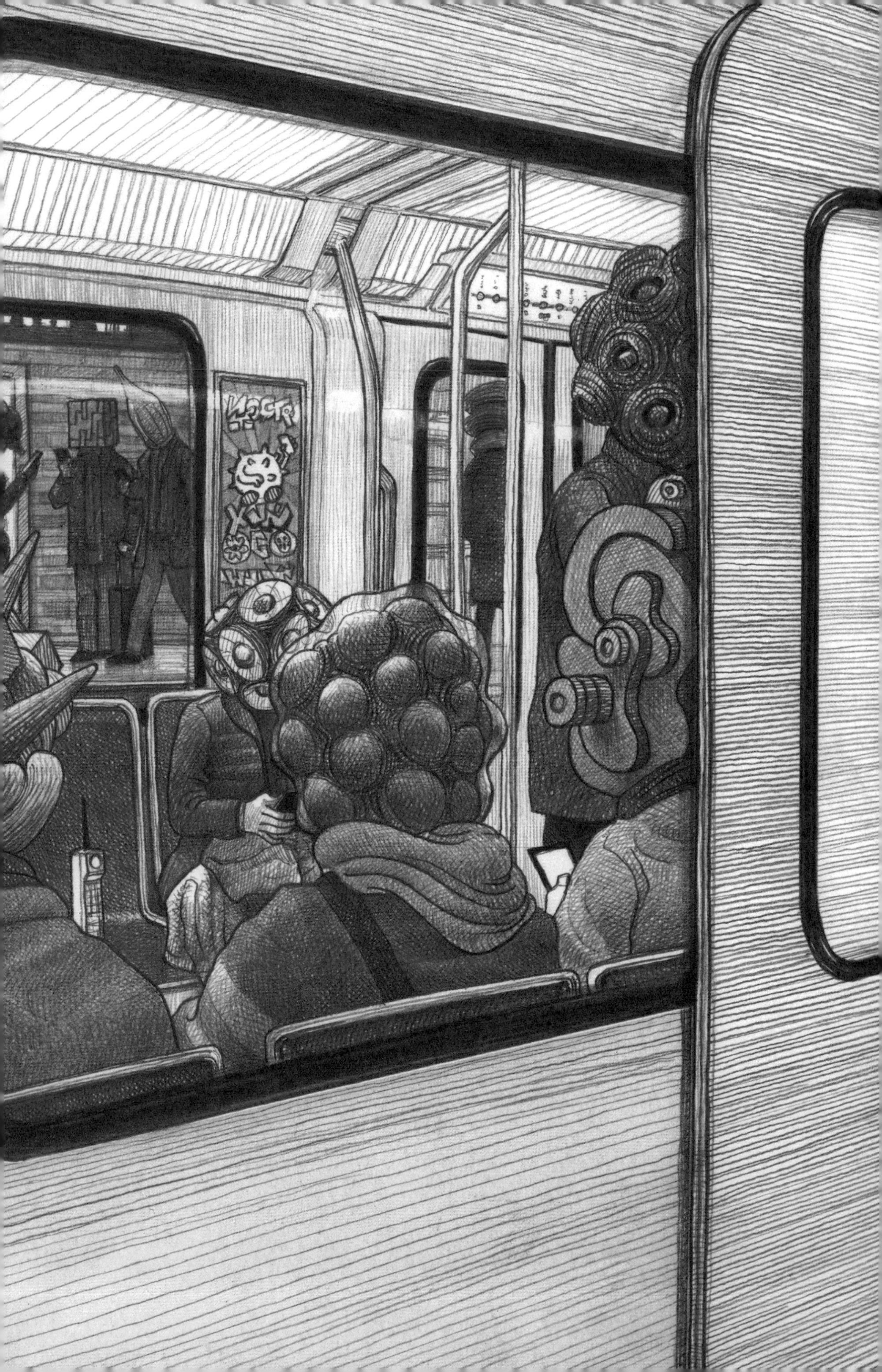

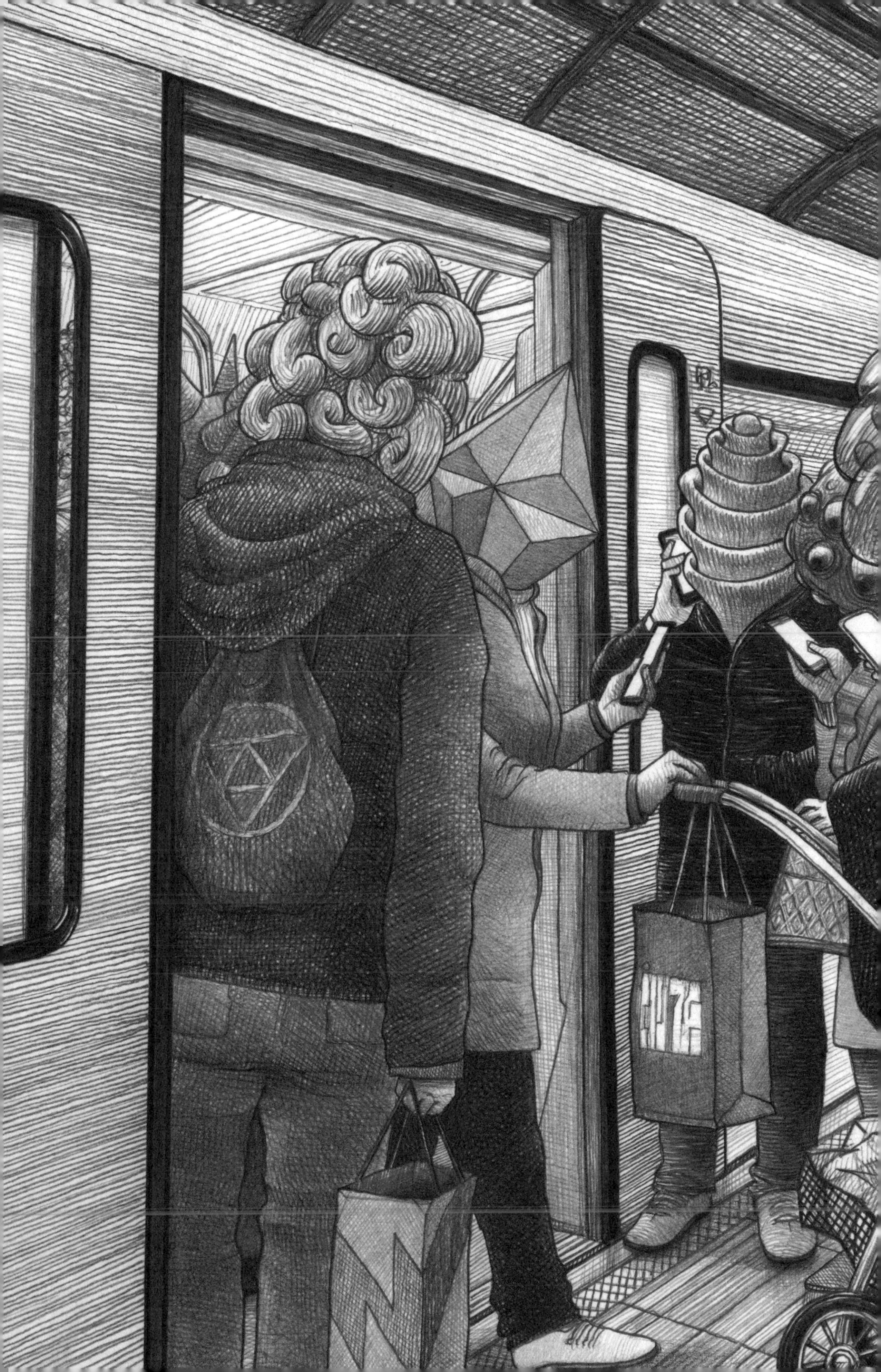

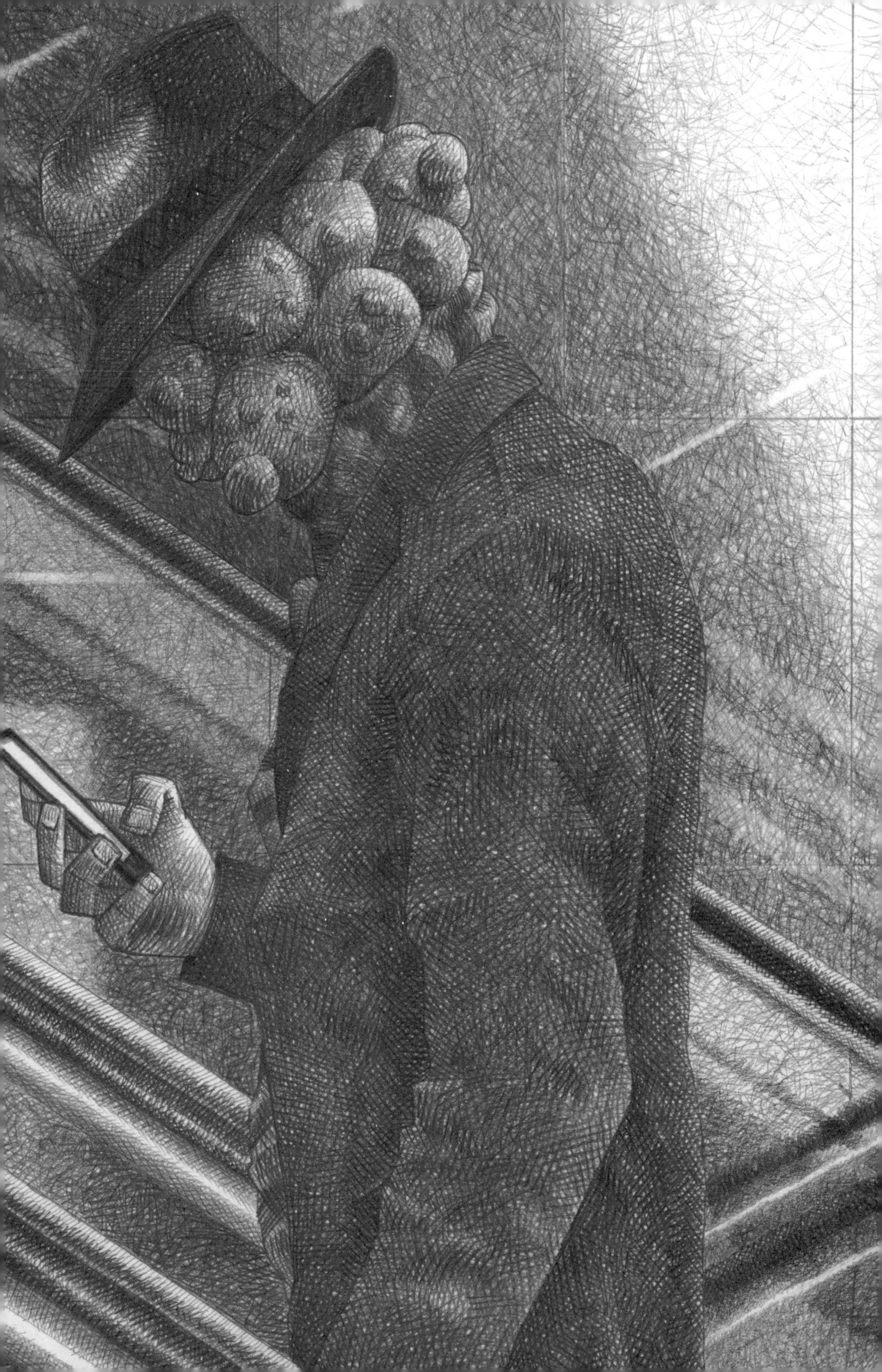

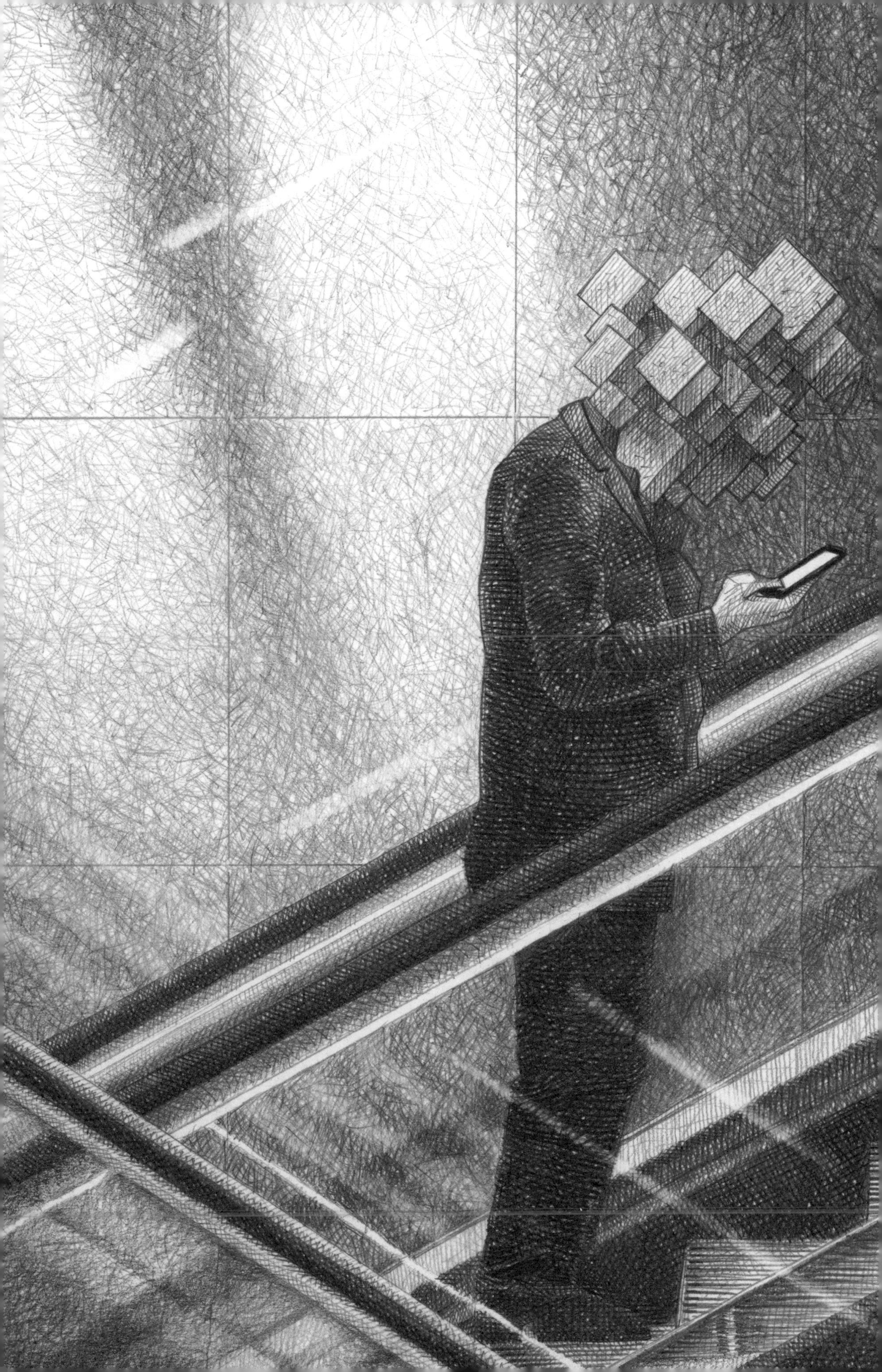

This is an Em Querido book
Published by Levine Querido

LQ
LEVINE QUERIDO

www.levinequerido.com · info@levinequerido.com
Levine Querido is distributed by Chronicle Books LLC

Originally published in Mexico by Alboroto Ediciones

Library of Congress Control Number: 2020940322
ISBN 978-1-64614-038-1

Printed and bound in China

FSC www.fsc.org MIX Paper from responsible sources FSC™ C104723

Published in April 2021
First Printing

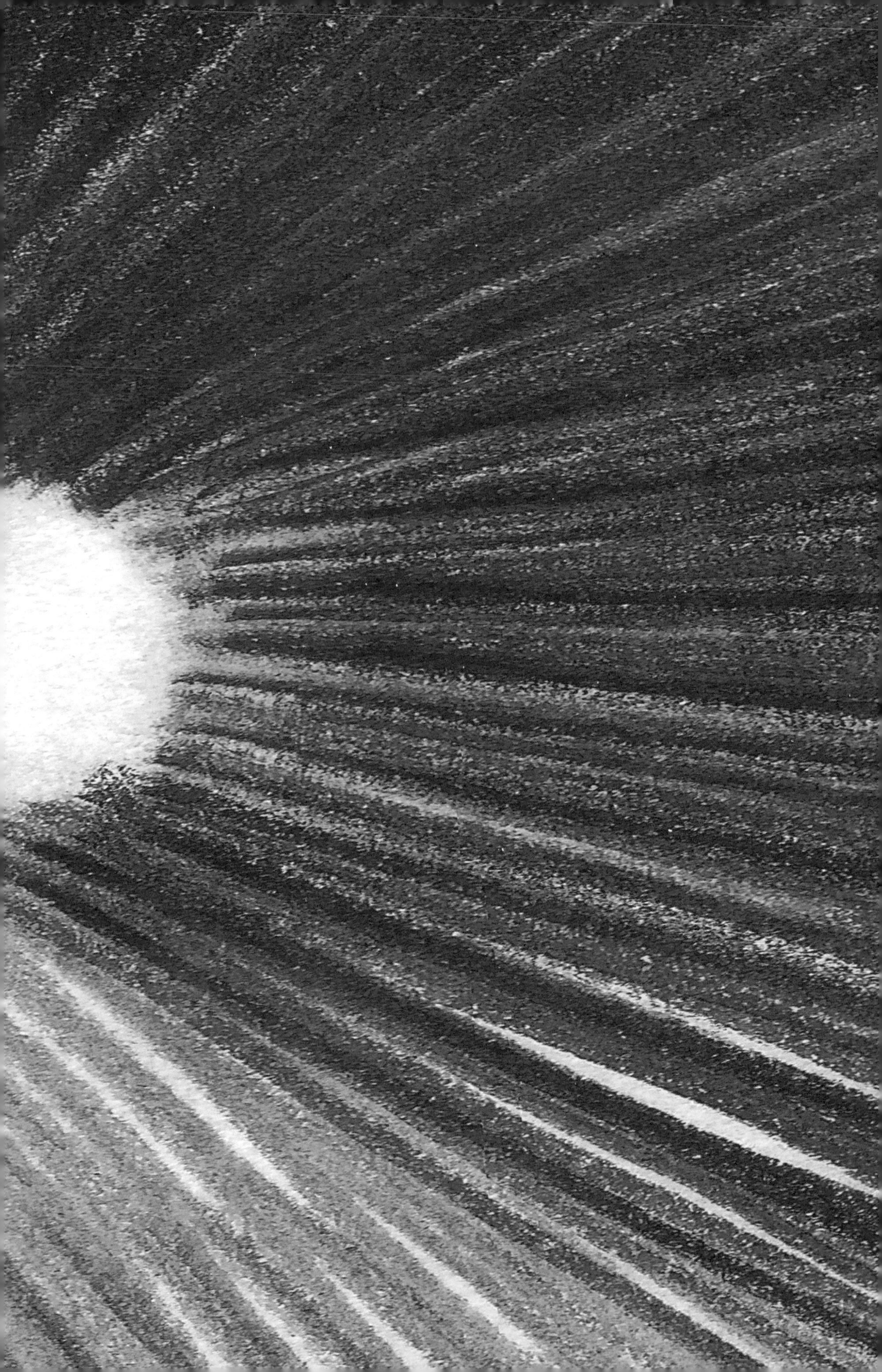